WANTED

Tired of endless days on the trail and the constant threat of sudden death, bounty hunter Duel Winston decided on the final bounty of his career before he called it quits. But John Barlow was a ruthless killer, the likes of which the West had never known. Lured to Tumbleweed, the ghost town that bore silent witness to Barlow's reign of terror, Winston found himself trapped in a life or death battle that threatened to send him into retirement — permanently.

Books by Lance Howard
in the Linford Western Library:

THE COMANCHE'S GHOST
THE WEST WITCH
THE GALLOWS GHOST
THE WIDOW MAKER
GUNS OF THE PAST
PALOMITA
THE LAST DRAW
THE DEADLY DOVES

LANCE HOWARD

WANTED

Complete and Unabridged

LINFORD
Leicester

First published in Great Britain in 1996 by
Robert Hale Limited
London

First Linford Edition
published 2001
by arrangement with
Robert Hale Limited
London

British Library CIP Data

Howard, Lance
Wanted.—Large print ed.—
Linford western library
1. Western stories
2. Large type books
I. Title
823.9′14 [F]

ISBN 0–7089–9734–1

Published by
F. A. Thorpe (Publishing)
Anstey, Leicestershire

Set by Words & Graphics Ltd.
Anstey, Leicestershire
Printed and bound in Great Britain by
T. J. International Ltd., Padstow, Cornwall

This book is printed on acid-free paper

For:
Walter Gibson and his mysterious
Shadow . . .

1

The Starr .36 was single action with a narrow base and six shots and shopkeeper Charlie Juzek got an entirely too close look at it.

Charlie, a shade into middle age, sporting an iron-flecked beard and receding hairline, felt sweat trickle from his forehead and zig-zag down his cheek. It itched. Powerfully. He had an overwhelming desire to swipe it away, but his hands, held high above his head, refused to move. The Starr was jammed between and a notch above his widened eyes. He stood stock still, as the man behind the gun let a sneer touch his lips. Charlie couldn't decide which boogered him more — the gun or the man.

The man had dirty brown hair, matted and tangled and sticking out from beneath a Stetson with a chip

— from a bullet — missing from one corner. A widow's peak stabbed deep into his creased forehead. His skin, deeply tanned and leathery, looked little different from a worn saddle. The only variance in shade was two roundish white patches the size of dimes on either cheek — remnants of where a bullet had burrowed through one side and out the other. The most distinguishing, and possibly the most frightening, aspect to his demeanor was his eyes, Nearly colorless, they imbued the man with an unnerving quality, as if his body were empty of soul.

Charlie instantly recognized the man from the Wanted posters, and being empty of soul damn near fitted the ticket.

'Wha-what do you want?' Charlie managed to stammer after a moment of pregnant silence. His bladder ached and he prayed a silent prayer he'd make it home to his wife and kids tonight, instead of winding up the way most of the man's victims did.

The man grinned. His eyes narrowed, devoid of any compassion, in fact filled with a peculiar burst of glee. From all accounts the man reveled in his work, took maniacal pleasure in robbing, killing and the like. Least that's what Charlie had read in the papers and now wasn't the time to debate the issue.

The outlaw pulled the Starr away from Charlie's forehead, leaving a whitened ring embedded into the flesh. Charlie, feeling only marginally relieved to have the piece off his person, realized it was mostly the man who boogered him. Charlie had been around guns, in fact owned a Peacemaker and scattergun, both hidden beneath the counter, but had not had experience with men the reputation of John Barlow, a hardcase who devastated entire towns and left trails of bodies in his wake.

John Barlow uttered a throaty chuckle and moved around the small area of the store, eyeing shelves crowded with packets and canned goods, sacks of grain and bottles of elixirs for nearly every damned ailment a body could muster. He paused, selecting a bottle and examining it.

'What's it say?' Barlow asked, glancing at the storekeep. 'I ain't so good with big words.'

Charlie gulped, suddenly noticing the bulge of a knife hilt tucked into Barlow's belt. 'It's . . . it's an elixir for the rheumatism.'

'Is it, now?' Barlow turned the bottle over in his hand. 'Reckon it works?'

'Of . . . course, of course it works.' A tremor laced the 'keep's voice. He wondered what the outlaw was leading up to. 'You didn't come here for no health problem.' Charlie felt amazed he mustered the courage to say that and instantly sorry when he saw the stormy look race across the outlaw's pale eyes.

'No, old man, reckon I didn't at that.' Barlow uttered a chopped laugh. Without warning he hurled the bottle at a mirror hanging above the counter.

The bottle shattered the glass with a jangle as loud as a shot. Shards rained on to the floor and Barlow laughed louder. Charlie shook, fighting to control his terror.

Barlow took a step towards him. 'None of this stuff works a lick — why you sell it?'

Charlie shook his head, unable to find the words. The outlaw was toying with him, a spider about to pull the legs off a fly.

'No matter.' Barlow waved the Starr. 'Like you said, I didn't come here for no health problem. Reckon it's way too late for that. Reckon it's way too late for you.'

A chill shuddered down Charlie's spine. He knew he was staring Death in the face. He had always wondered what would happen if that day came; he suspected all along it would, but had forced the thought to the back of his mind. The territory was wild out here, just spitting distance 'cross the New Mex border. Men died routinely, usually young and usually with violence. His wife called him a fool for wanting to move West to start this business and by damn he had to admit, in his last moments of life, she was right, especially with men the likes of John Barlow running free. Hell, Charlie had heard the outlaw had turned a town not so far from here — Tumbleweed, if he recollected right — into a ghost town, and no lawman appeared especially eager to buck him. Charlie said another prayer, one he reckoned was futile but one he needed to say just the same: if God let him out of this, let him live, he promised he'd ride hellbent back to St Louis, say *adios* to this God-forsaken parcel of land.

'You can t-take all the money — it's in the safe . . . please, please I have a wife and kids.'

'Don't they all?' Barlow's lips tightened. 'Oh, I aim to take all the money, old man, but it's more than that, yessir, it shorely is.'

'Wha-what do you mean?'

Barlow tilted his head. 'You know who I am?'

Charlie nodded. 'B-Barlow, John Barlow.'

'Good, I like it when they know. Makes killin' more fun. Reckon I like the recognition. Like bein' known and havin' nobody able to lift a finger to stop me. Makes my blood burn, old man.'

'Someone will stop you . . . '

'Yeah? Who? You? Ain't likely. The sheriff? Hell, he saw me ride in and scooted right back into his hidey-hole. Probably got the door locked and hidin' under his desk by now.'

'You sonofabitch!' Charlie said it knowing full well he was going to die, but deciding to pass with dignity. John Barlow brought fear and death, and while death appeared inevitable, fear was not. Charlie felt boogered all right; no doubt about that, but he was determined not to back down to the hardcase in his last moments. He would leave this world with a fight.

Charlie formed the thought to charge

Barlow, even felt his body tense for motion. Barlow must have sensed it because suddenly the butt of the Starr streaked towards Charlie's jaw.

It connected and pain rattled through Charlie's teeth. Blood from his mashed lip spattered across his boiled shirt. The small room did a jig and Charlie felt his senses waver.

Another blow! The side of the Starr bounced off his temple. Charlie felt his legs go in different directions. He went backwards and down, crashing into a shelf. Cans tumbled from the shelf and clattered about him, rolling. He looked up with blurry vision, the fight draining from him.

Barlow leaned close. 'You got sand, old man. Ain't gonna do you a hell of a lot of good, but I admire it. Reckon it's something I never had till I learned to take it.' Barlow grinned. 'I'll do you a favor and make your death right quick for it — right after you tell me the combination to that old safe you got in the back . . . '

* * *

No See, Colorado, came into view in the distance and Duel Winston realized where the town had picked up its name. It was a speck in the barren vista of sage and dust. It reminded him of a hangnail, an ugly half-moon affair of shabby buildings, a stopover for those who journeyed from points east, seeking their share of New Mexico's riches of gold, silver, turquoise and sin. It squatted a half-day's ride from the border of New Mexico Territory and like many such towns, Duel reckoned No See wouldn't exist in a few years — unless it hit it lucky, way that other desert town he'd heard tell of west of here, Las-something-or-other.

No See was a town he might never have given a second look had he not a job to do.

A job. That's what he called it, nowadays. In the past it had been an ambition, a dream, a driven thing, sterling and virginal as the frontier itself. A burning desire brought about by circumstances dealt him by the Devil. A greenhorn, aglow with the prospects of making the West a safer place, fueled by the kerosene taste of revenge. He dispensed justice, killing those who deserved no better, those who preyed on the innocent. That's how he had started out. Years had eroded that nobleness, tarnished it like the silver dream it had been. A thin layer of silver prettying up the corrosion that lay beneath. He wondered what the hell had happened to him to make him feel so disillusioned. Was it a specific incident? A gradual thing? Maybe it was the constant death, the killing, the trail of bodies. Maybe all the black souls haunted him. Somehow, when he started this thing, he envisioned it differently. He saw the outlaws giving themselves up at the first draw of his gun — make no mistake about it, he was controlled lightning with that piece, or at least had been. He had slipped a notch, he noticed, reflexes dulling just a hair. Maybe it was age, though dammit he wasn't old. A shade past thirty, maybe older in mind. More like he felt a plain flatness, a discontent eating its way out of his heart because of the damnable constancy of the thing. Every town more the same than not, every outlaw a black reflection of the one before. They rarely came peaceably; he had been a damn fool to ever think they would. Consistently, the hardcases challenged him, tested his mettle, always to their own demise. While bullets had grazed him — Lord knew he had more scars on his muscular frame than he could count — never had one pierced his vitals, or discouraged him enough to quit.

Why don't you quit?

The thought had plagued his mind more times than he cared to count and always he came back with the same answer: *I don't know*.

He wanted to quit. God knew he wanted to. He was sick of it, sick of the never-changing pattern: the chase, the inevitable cornering, the constant death. Sick to death of death, he told himself a thousand times over. Yet some dark force inside drove him onward, a bastard need he couldn't rightly fathom. How many sleepless nights had he pondered it? Hell, he'd lost track. He felt worn, like an old holster, worn and older than his time, but still he kept on.

He had another reason to quit, he recollected, the most important one: the reason that made him promise himself the two dodgers tucked in his saddle-bag would be his final bounties. One bounty a quick and easy payday, the other . . . well, a job that would finally, in his mind, provide him the means of fulfilment he needed, craved maybe, to put a cap on a career past its dyin' time. The most dangerous bounty he'd ever accepted.

Then he could go back to her.

How long had he unconsciously edged himself in her direction, a town a day's ride into New Mex Territory? He cursed his stubborn hide for leaving her in the first place. He should have married that gal instead of leaving her to ply her 'trade' instead of leaving her with the empty promise of a man always searching for something he might never find.

Unless he captured John Barlow.

Captured? Pshaw! Captured was not in the bounty-hunter's manual for a man like Barlow. Only violent death waited with an outlaw of that stature.

He drew up his bay, straightening in the saddle. He rolled his shoulders, which were sore and stiff, and sucked in a breath of heated air. Digging into his saddle-bags, he pulled out the dodgers, shoving one back into the bag and unfolding the other. He stared at the cruel features of the hardcase, Barlow, reminding himself why he had come to No See, the tip — hell, tip wasn't even the word. Damn near to everybody knew where Barlow could be found. The outlaw made a habit of showing himself, taunting the law, mocking it.

Duel saw a bit of the actor in the hardcase, a bit he prayed would lead to the killer's downfall.

As with most of Barlow's ilk, the hardcase had grown cocky, full of himself. He appeared to enjoy the recognition and infamy. That might give Duel an edge, sharpen the part of him that had dulled. Yet he could not afford the same sense of cockiness, let it cause him to misjudge the hardcase: Barlow was deadly, deadlier than anyone Duel had tracked. He reckoned it had been only a matter of time before someone got around to the notion of hiring him to bring Barlow to justice. He had expected it, kept it simmering in the back of his mind, and when that day had come he had felt a peculiar sense of relief. Seems Barlow had murdered the daughter of a wealthy railroad man up Wyoming way after having his way with her. The railroad owner unlike many had overcome his fear and decided to take steps in sealing the demise of the outlaw. The railroad man had settled on the only man good enough — or loco enough — to track the hardcase.

Duel Winston.

Duel folded the dodger and shoved it into his pocket. He lifted his hat, tugging free the bandanna from his neck and wiping grime and sweat from his brow. His longish brown hair, matted and soaked with sweat, stuck out from beneath the hat when he replaced it. He had a solid jaw covered with two days beard growth. Premature lines creased his young face. His brown eyes narrowed to a squint under the harsh glare of the sun. He'd spent two days in the saddle, riding from the last town Barlow had visited. The heat felt stinging and his mouth felt arid, his skin dried as parchment. Another aspect of his career he'd grown tired of. Only the knowledge Barlow was headed to No See spurred him past his ennui.

Was the hardcase still in No See? Maybe. Or maybe he had moved on. It didn't matter because Duel would find him. John Barlow was a man who made little secret of his whereabouts while proving elusive to the few brave — or stupid — souls who dared follow him. Of course those men were dead. Duel knew that, and it gave him pause, though he was bullheaded enough to ignore it.

He reckoned the day was fast approaching when he would be the one they buried. It was the manhunter's lot when that edge dulled. He knew it and lived with it. But if all went according to plan, he would finish these last two jobs and think on it no longer.

But things had a way of veering off plan when it came to men like John Barlow.

He gigged his horse towards the town, a foreboding flutter of nerves in his belly telling him he was close to the outlaw, that the hardcase hadn't moved on yet. He felt strangely excited and hesitant at the same time for reasons he couldn't pinpoint. He always did at the end of the trail . . .

The bay's hooves gouged into the

trail and dust billowed around him, coating his lips and settling a film over his clothes and gloves. The town swelled before him and at the mouth of No See he reined up, studying the ramshackle buildings and sighing. The flutter in his belly strengthened.

He's here . . .

The thought came unbidden and sure. He's here. He's here and the moment you've known would come finally has. Destiny, some might call it, but Duel preferred to label it fate. For destiny carried an assumed conclusion of achievement while fate carried one of finality. And death. Duel reckoned that was a whole hell of a lot closer to the case here.

He eased his Winchester .44-40 from its saddleboot and checked its load, then reholstered the rifle. He drew his Peacemaker .45 from the greased holster thonged to his thigh. He peered down its barrel, its sight filed down to prevent snagging in a quick draw. He eyed the hair trigger, sensitive to his skilled touch, then slid a bullet into the empty sixth chamber. Reholstering the gun, he breathed deeply, fighting to ease the tension in his muscular frame. His hand drifted to the bowie knife sheathed at his side, feeling its comforting bulge.

He heeled the horse into a slow walk, eyes searching the street, the shoddily constructed buildings — saloon, sheriff's office, scattered shops. The streets were practically deserted, the few men moving about the dusty boardwalks carrying drawn looks and an air of skittishness. Duel recognized the look — the same look that stained every town in the throes of death.

Had Barlow come and gone? You'd think so from the looks he got, but this was one thing John Barlow likely couldn't accept credit for. No See was wasting away of its own bad planning and something about that made Duel feel somber and resigned. If he were indeed fated to die at the hands of Barlow, he vowed it would never be in a place like this.

What are you talking death for? he

scolded himself. It wasn't like him. Death always found those he hunted, didn't it? He was always a hair quicker on the draw, a step ahead. Why should it be any different this time?

He uttered a pained laugh, shaking his head. Maybe you are getting old after all, he told himself. Or maybe something in the cards told him today just wasn't his day.

He drew up in front of the sheriff's office and dismounted, gaze scanning the street a final time, looking for anything out of place. The scene struck him as entirely too quiet, as if a dark cloud had swallowed No See, weighted it with dread. He had sensed that in other towns he'd tracked Barlow through, so maybe he was too late.

He crossed the boardwalk and opened the office door. At first he saw no one inside. The interior was dark after being out in the bright sunlight and his eyes needed a moment to adjust. His gaze lifted, spotting a man keeping close to the back of the room, nearly out of sight.

Duel stepped deeper into the room, an air of caution taking him. Something was wrong, bad wrong, and a warning bell clanged in his head.

'You the sheriff?' he asked, cocking his head.

The man edged forward, the star on his breast catching a glint of sunlight arcing through the window.

'Who are you?' the sheriff asked and Duel suddenly saw the fear in the man's eyes, the rigid set of his body. The man was dead boogered, in Duel's opinion, and like a winter wind a notion howled through him.

'Where is he?' Duel asked, voice controlled.

'W-who?' The sheriff shuddered, eyelids fluttering.

Duel had neither the time nor patience for games. As sure as he knew the sun had risen in the east this morning he knew John Barlow was still in No See. The sheriff's manner told him that much.

Duel grabbed the sheriff by the shirt. 'Godammit! You better tell me 'fore I decide to take you with me lookin' for him!' Duel pressed his face close, features twisted with fury. The sheriff had a large yellow streak. The man had no call being a lawman and likely would end up dying for it.

'He-he's over to the general store, been there a few minutes. I saw him ride in.'

Duel shoved the man back, throwing him against the desk and drawing his Peacemaker. 'What the hell kind of a lawman are you? If the shopkeep's in there Barlow will kill him. How could you let that happen?'

'I . . . I . . . '. The sheriff's mouth made fish movements but no further words came out. He trembled and Duel shook his head in disgust.

'I oughta shoot you myself!' Duel spun and headed back out onto the boardwalk.

So Barlow was here. This was it. It all came down to this moment and soon he would have the answer he'd been searching for: or he'd be dead. He could see it no other way.

He squinted with the brightness, scanning the street. The general store. Two blocks down. Barlow was there and by all prospects a shopkeeper occupied the store with him. Dead or alive? Duel prayed alive. He'd deal with the death of the outlaw, but an innocent man . . . he had little belly for that.

Edging across the street, he pressed close to the buildings. Scooting two blocks, he halted before the window of the general store and peered through.

He saw the outlaw hit the storekeep, then pistol whip him in the temple. The 'keep went down, but he was alive and Duel thanked Heaven for that much.

Seeing the outlaw in person, a larger man than the dodger had indicated, he felt a strange sense of deadness flood his innards. It was that way whenever he caught up with his quarry. Something cold, something calculating, took over. His nerves turned to ice and his reflexes became precision. A sense of grimness gripped his mind.

A sudden movement from the side grabbed his attention. He looked up to see a woman step around the corner on to the boardwalk. She was blonde, attractive but hard-looking. She wore a bar dress, bosom swelled above a red santeen bodice. For an instant he saw another woman standing there, a woman he longed for. This woman much resembled her, but the illusion quickly dissolved, leaving a sunny wanting in his heart.

Her hard eyes settled on him and he raised a finger to his lips, signaling silence. She gave him a peculiar look and seemed about to say something, but didn't. She stood stock still and he felt a sting of hesitancy for a reason he couldn't pinpoint. He forced it away and edged in front of the window, crouching, Peacemaker ready. He had little time to consider the girl. The 'keep was alive, but wouldn't be in another moment.

The door was open a fraction and Duel drew a deep breath. He leaped forward, kicking it inward and leveling the .45 in the same movement.

'Barlow!' he yelled, filling the doorway. Barlow froze and Duel waited for that split second in time, that hint of movement and intent telling him Barlow would spin, bring his gun around for that inevitable last-ditch attempt to escape capture. It happened damn near every time and Duel had to admit the situation couldn't have been more to his advantage. Barlow was half-turned, half-crouched, in poor position to get off the first shot. Duel saw only one move Barlow could make to throw the odds off kilter. He could shoot the shopkeep and though Duel would kill the outlaw it would prove a hollow victory in a way because an innocent man would die.

He got a surprise. Barlow did neither.

'Who are you?' the outlaw asked, voice low, almost demanding.

'Duel Winston.' Duel waited for the

indication of movement, the trick some outlaws used of coming up shooting in mid-sentence, but it never came.

'Bounty hunter?'

'Of a sorts. Peacemaker might be more accurate.'

'Manhunter with a sense of humor . . . I like that.' Barlow dropped his gun. The Starr clattered on the floorboards and Barlow straightened, turning, hands slightly raised.

Duel couldn't have been more shocked. Of every option his mind had concocted over the last days in the saddle, the weeks of tracking Barlow, this was one he had never imagined: the outlaw surrendering. It struck him as suddenly wrong. A tingling in his nerves, an inbred sense told him things just weren't right. Barlow shouldn't have surrendered. It wasn't like his type, not at all, but damned if Duel could see what he was up to. A man with the reputation of Barlow just giving up . . . it made no sense.

'Move away from him,' Duel ordered,

gesturing with the Peacemaker. 'And kick the gun over here.'

Barlow gave a chopped laugh and complied. He kicked the Starr to Duel and stepped back.

Duel scooched, pinning his sights on Barlow all the while, and picked up the gun. He shoved it into his belt.

The shopkeep recovered and pushed himself to his feet, babbling. 'God, mister, I'm mighty glad — '

'Shut the hell up!' Barlow snapped, gazing at the 'keep, who clamped his mouth shut. 'I gave you credit for sand, don't change my opinion of you by blubbering.'

'Ain't likely it matters, now, Barlow,' Duel said. 'Looks to me like he ain't the only one with a streak of yellow.' Duel smirked, still puzzling over the outlaw giving himself up and hoping cowardice was it.

Barlow chuckled. 'Yellow ain't in my nature no more, bounty man.' He nudged his head at Duel. 'You got more balls than most. No other bounty hunter'd be damn fool 'nough to come after me.'

'Seems like they should have long ago; would've saved a lot of killin'. You ain't as much as your reputation makes you out to be.'

'Reputations are ghosts, bounty man. Here there's only you and me and fate.'

Duel tensed a fraction. Strange Barlow should use that word: fate. For an instant he felt as if he were gazing at a bastard reflection of himself, a reflection of what he might have become had he been born without a soul. Was he so far removed from that? Each man delivered sudden violent death, one on the side of justice the other on the side of lawlessness.

'You ain't cut out for this business no more, bounty man. I can read it on your face. You're lookin' to get out. I can make that easy for you. Just let me walk out that door and you can just quit.'

'If I don't?' Duel's body tightened another notch. The outlaw unnerved him, reading him so accurately, and he didn't care for it a lick.

Barlow grinned. 'I'll haunt you . . . '.

'Move out,' Duel ordered, gesturing with the Peacemaker. He stepped back, giving Barlow a clear path to the door.

'What you intend doin' with me?'

'You'll sit tight in a cell at the sheriff's and I'll wait till further law arrives. Don't reckon I can trust what this town's got.'

Barlow's grin widened. 'You got that right, bounty man.'

Barlow moved towards the door, stepped out on to the boardwalk. Duel came directly behind him, alert for any sign of a trick.

But not alert enough.

The feeling of wrongness plaguing him suddenly came home. Barlow's arm flashed up in a sweeping motion and Duel realized the bargirl he'd seen on the way in had been standing beside the doorway, looking in. The hardcase grabbed her, yanked her around, a knife appearing in his hand from somewhere beneath his coat. The blade pressed into the soft flesh of her throat and she let out a bleat. Duel froze, belly sinking.

'Like I said, bounty man, you and me and fate. And this here little lady is mine.' He jammed the blade harder against the girl's throat, though not hard enough to draw blood.

Duel kept the Peacemaker leveled, unsure of his next move for one of the few times in his life. A single mistake would cause the girl's death; he would have no way to save her. But if he let Barlow take her, would her chances be any better?

Again a feeling of wrongness took him. The girl had been standing there too long, showing too much interest in the proceedings, as if she were waiting to be captured. But why? Was he misreading the situation? Had she been merely curious, in the wrong place at the wrong time? Or was she in league with Barlow? He had heard no reports of such a thing, but that didn't rule out the possibility.

'My gun . . . ' Barlow said, nudging his head at Duel's belt. 'Then you're gonna let me ride on out of here or I'll give the lady an extra mouth. Your choice, bounty man . . . '

Duel took a step closer, halted. If she were in cahoots with the hardcase she was in no danger. But if she were innocent, a wrong move on his part would make him responsible for her death. He couldn't take that chance.

Duel eased the Starr out of his belt and, crouching, placed it on the boardwalk.

'Step back into that store and close the door,' Barlow ordered.

Duel's face set in grim lines as he complied. He saw the 'keep scurry back into the store behind him. He shut the door, watching Barlow through the dusty window.

The outlaw came forward, keeping the girl before him, and picked up his gun, holstering it.

'You follow me, bounty man and

she's on your conscience!' Barlow yelled, jerking the girl backward and disappearing around the corner.

Duel grabbed the doorhandle and swung it open, scooting out into the street. The thunder of hoofbeats grabbed his attention.

The outlaw, girl in the saddle in front of him, blasted out into the street. They raced for the end of town, a cloud of dust billowing behind them. He could have shot the outlaw in the back but he stood too big a chance of Barlow killing the girl if only wounded. Duel couldn't be sure his shot at a moving target would be true enough to stop the outlaw dead.

Frustration eating him, he watched as the hardcase made his escape. It was a first for him, and now he saw why Barlow had proved elusive prey. Duel had sensed something off kilter and it had been. Barlow was gone and that prolonged the inevitable. They would meet again; Duel saw little choice there. Would the outlaw have the advantage next time? Barlow surely knew Duel would come for him.

'Damn . . . ' Duel whispered, watching the dust settle in the street.

2

John Barlow had escaped. But where had he gone? The question had haunted Duel Winston since yesterday, when the outlaw outwitted him and vanished into the western vista.

Duel sat atop his bay, searching the horizon, which shimmered with heat waves. The waves distorted the panorama of scrub brush and sage, dust and scattered shards of rock. Everything took on a strange moving pattern, nightmarish in the bright blazing day. The brassy sun beat down on him yet a chill slithered along his spine. Mopping his brow with his bandanna, he cursed the day, the surroundings and John Barlow.

And himself.

You are slipping. You have to be or Barlow wouldn't have escaped. You would have put a bullet through his black heart the way you have countless other hardcases. What the hell's the matter with you?

Another question haunted him: he felt virtually positive the bargirl was in league with Barlow, planted outside the store for just such a contingency. Yet he had hesitated, unsure, unable to risk a life on his indecisiveness. He recollected a day when he would have challenged the hardcase, called his bluff. But he had changed without knowing exactly how. He *had* lost that edge all manhunters needed to survive, that sixth sense that told him what was right and what was wrong, what was real and what was bluff.

Duel felt Death stalking him, waiting for him around every corner. He felt it deep in his bones like the coming of a blue norther, yet darker, more threatening. He needed that edge one last time if he intended to finish what he started — the downfall of John Barlow. And make no mistake, he had no choice but to finish it. If he didn't, Barlow would.

He had seen it in the hardcase's eyes when he held the girl, a promise: I'll find you again, bounty man. I'll find you and things will be different.

Duel couldn't afford to let that happen. While he had toyed with the idea of giving it all up, now, going back to *her*, he could no longer consider the notion until Barlow was in a cell or beneath the ground.

Duel preferred the latter.

Barlow had few options as well, Duel figured. That's what had set Duel on the trail to Burton's Bend, a small town spitting distance 'cross the New Mex border. From No See you went either north or south, and the few signs Duel had read along the trail plainly indicated Barlow had ridden south. The first town in that direction was Burton's Bend. That suited Duel just fine. The marshal there was an acquaintance of his and Duel could use that to his advantage. If Barlow somehow made it past that town . . . well, beyond Burton's Bend was . . .

Her.

Duel shuddered at the thought. He preferred Barlow didn't make it that far, put her in danger in any way. There was always the chance Barlow would veer off and head to the next town, a parcel of nowhere he had made infamous by turning it into a ghost town: Tumbleweed. If that were the case, fewer innocent folks stood to get dead.

Duel wrestled with his thoughts, lips drawing tight as he continued scanning the horizon, seeking a glimpse of Burton's Bend. He had been riding a hair over an hour, but already he was tired of the saddle. His belly felt full of lead and his nerves felt raw. Another sign of age creeping in: impatience. In his line of work that was a commodity he could ill afford.

Duel gigged the bay into motion, riding at a steady clip. He tasted the dust in his mouth, gritty, savory as a prospector's vittles. It clogged his throat and nostrils and he dreamed of the day he could settle in one place where he would not live coated with trail grime. The day he could be with her and know he was going to stay. Perhaps that day wasn't so far away. Perhaps it was never.

What if Barlow's not there and you misjudged him again? Duel had remained the night in No See, exhausted from his days on the trail. He was fresher, but he had lost time, enough time for Barlow to move on.

The thought intruded on his reverie. That was a possibility he had little desire to chew on. He would have laid bets Barlow knew he was being dogged and wouldn't be as brazen as in the past. Barlow wasn't used to having men come after him. If Duel read the hardcase correctly, that would make him more cautious, craftier; that gave Duel no comfort.

The miles melted away as the sun, brassy and scorching, rose higher in the crystal-blue sky. As Duel slipped deeper into thought, he caught glimpses of ghosts skittering within the heatwaves, the spectres of the men he had killed, outlaws all, deservedly dying, yet somehow leaving a bitter taste in his soul.

Who am I fooling? he asked himself. Did he somehow enjoy the killing, the surge of retribution that darted through his being at the end of a chase? Maybe he had become little more of a man than John Barlow. Maybe he had become an outlaw in his own right, one with merely a thread of humanity and conscience. A thread worn thin and close to snapping.

God help him if he had. God help John Barlow if he hadn't.

Burton's Bend suddenly loomed before his vision. His eyes stung with the sweat dripping from his brow and the town blurred, but he blew out a relieved sigh.

Was Barlow there?

He rode on, the town swelling. He recollected Burton's Bend fondly, the times he'd spent there, passing through on his way north. He recollected the ladies of Burton's Bend most of all and it shamed him in a way because now he would gladly give up every last one of them to be with . . . Samantha.

Well, that didn't matter at the moment. He couldn't let himself be distracted with thoughts of her. His edge was dulled enough.

He trotted the bay into town, gazing upon the familiar false fronts of buildings and offices. A larger town than No See, but not by a lot. One with life flowing sweet in its veins, built on more than false promises and pipe dreams. Built by men of iron muscle and steel will, men with a burning need for life and living. Burton's Bend was *alive* for all its iniquity — bargirls, gambling, an endless river of whiskey — yet with that iniquity it held true to a cleanness, a code. The marshal kept things in check and its vices were contained, a tonic instead of a drug. Fights occurred rarely, and killings tallied one or two a year — on a bad year. While the marshal viewed women, whiskey and wagering as legitimate outlets for hard-working men, he would not tolerate murder and suffering. Right or wrong, that was Burton's Bend. If there existed such a thing as clean sin, Burton's Bend had it. And Duel felt strangely at home there.

He slowed the bay as he rode along the wide main street, surveying the area. Folks moved about freely along the boardwalk; no ripple of tenseness hindered their stride, no pinched fear stained their faces.

He's not here . . .

Duel felt his hopes sink. If Barlow were in Burton's Bend wouldn't there be that subdued sense of terror that plagued other towns he had devastated? Duel would have thought so, yet . . .

Doubt surfaced in his mind, something he couldn't pinpoint. A whisper of that sixth sense? He reckoned so. Maybe his edge had sharpened and maybe John Barlow held the whetstone.

He gave his study another few

minutes, unable to pick out anything off kilter or any clue to indicate Barlow lurked nearby. Still he used caution as he stepped from his saddle, after drawing up in front of the marshal's office. He checked his Peacemaker and Winchester's loads, keeping the horse between his body and the front of the street, so as not to present a clean target for anyone looking to surprise him. He glanced at rooftops, catching no glint of sun from gun metal and almost relaxed. Almost. Relaxing was another thing he reckoned he'd have to relearn once this was over.

He stepped across the boardwalk and entered the office, pausing just inside the door to let his eyes adjust to the gloom. A man sat behind the desk, shuffling through a stack of Wanted dodgers.

'Hear you got the cleanest rooms in town . . . ' Duel said. A personal joke between them, from a remark the lawman had made about having clean cells because he never had to use them.

The marshal looked up, a smile pulling at his lips. He was a rugged man, beefy as a longhorn, with hands strong enough to bend horseshoes. Duel had seen him demonstrate the feat and the thought of it still amazed him. Greying hair receded from a creased forehead and his face sported a reddish-bronze look of too much sun.

'Duel Winston, as I live and breathe!' Ben Morrison said with gusto, heaving out of his chair and moving around the desk. The marshal shoved out a hand and Duel took it, almost wincing at the grip.

'As I recollect, you were the one who said I probably wouldn't be living and breathing the next time you saw me.'

'Whelp, you got that one right. You're the kinda fella you constantly expect to see come in in the back of a wagon, what in your line of business an' all. Awfully glad you came in here on your own two legs!'

'That makes two of us . . . '. Duel lifted his hat and wiped his brow.

The marshal laughed and went to a wooden table holding a coffee pot. He grabbed two tin cups, swiped dust from their interiors with a bandanna, and poured coffee into them. He passed one to Duel. 'Arbuckle's best . . . '. He lifted his cup to his lips.

Duel sipped at the coffee, which was cold, as the marshal angled around his desk and sat. Duel lowered himself into a chair in front of the desk, leaning back and making a face. 'Gawd, Ben, strong enough to take the rust off an iron fence!'

'That's the way I like my coffee.'

'And your whiskey, if I recollect right.'

Ben Morrison nodded. 'Not to mention my women!'

A moment of silence weighted the room. Duel felt himself searching for something to say, but the time for small talk had passed.

Ben Morrison saved him the trouble. 'You got the look of a man bent on findin' himself something, Duel. I seen that look on you before, back when you chased down the last member of the Cayton gang.'

Duel nodded, uncomfortable for a reason he couldn't pinpoint. 'Thought that would be my toughest case.'

'Thought it would be your last, 'specially when you met that little filly. She loved you, Duel. Any fool could tell that. You shoulda gone an' stayed with her, if you don't mind my sayin' it.'

I loved her, Duel thought, but didn't voice it. Ben Morrison was right; Duel couldn't argue or deny it. Her face rose in his mind and the blade of remorse and lonesomeness stabbed his heart. He forced the image away, sighing.

'Reckon you're right, and I plan to — '

'You always plan to, Duel. Hell, you planned it then an' you probably planned it a hunnert times. What makes today any different?'

Duel felt himself bristle, but knew the lawman was merely trying to goad him into settling on something he truly desired. 'It'll be different this time; you'll have to take my word on it.'

'Your word's good enough with me, Duel.' Ben Morrison leaned forward, eyeing him. 'But is it good enough with you?'

'It has to be. Soon as I get these two jobs done, I'm quitting.'

'I hope so, son. I shorely hope so. You're a good man, Duel Winston, but you're spittin' in the face of the Devil. All bounty hunters do and they all either wind up with hearts hard as stone or their boots up.'

'I'll try to keep that in mind.' Duel felt eager to change the subject and was glad when Morrison did.

'So what brings you back this way — less you're headin' towards her town . . . '.

Morrison had come closer to the truth than he might have thought. Duel dug into a pocket and pulled out the folded dodger. Unfolding it, he tossed it on the desk and Morrison swung it around.

'Chris'a'mighty! John Barlow!' Morrison shook his head, pushing back the dodger as if it were on fire. 'You got a death wish, now?'

Maybe . . .

'Reckon I don't. But John Barlow does, far as I'm concerned. He's the one I've been looking for all my life maybe, the excuse I need to say I done it all and can give it up.'

'Hell, don't go foolin' yourself. John Barlow ain't known for leaving a body alive and you, good as you are, ain't likely to stop that trend.'

'He'll make a mistake. They all do. And when it comes I'll be ready for it.'

'Will you?'

Duel folded the dodger and tucked it back in his pocket then folded his arms. 'Damn right. I got that filly waitin' on me after all!' His attempt at lightening the mood failed.

'If she ain't got tireda frettin' about you bein' killed everyday.'

'She's . . . a hell of a woman. Strong enough for that.'

'Ain't no woman strong enough for that. Maybe at first, but after a spell it wears on you.'

Morrison could well have been right; that fact gnawed at Duel. Maybe Sam wouldn't be waiting. Hell, it had been what? Over a year since the Cayton job. She might have gotten fed up spending her days frettin' over a man as holdable as the wind, as likely to live out his days as a jack-rabbit in a coyote's den. She met men, hundreds of them in her line of work, all with more to offer than a man like him, a man haunted by a never-done job and ever-shifting spaces. Maybe a man who belonged nowhere.

'Dammit, Ben, you got a way of annoying me!' Duel tried to put a laugh behind the words, but the effort fell short.

'Reckon I do and I'll keep at it till you make good on your word to yourself.'

'I will, I promise.'

'Right after you corral John Barlow, right?'

'Him and a minor job after that.'

Morrison blew out a grunt of disgust. 'Never changes. Makes me wonder why I count you as a friend when you could be buried the next moment.'

'Must be my cheery personality.' Duel laughed. Morrison laughed, too, though the expression seemed strained.

'Reckon that's it.'

'You seen him?'

'Barlow?' Morrison's eyes widened. 'Hell, if I had I probably wouldn't be sittin' here jawin' at you. Most lawmen who see him don't live to tell about it; the ones that do are all in his pocket.'

'I think he came this way.'

'How so?'

Duel explained to him the events at No See and how he had trailed the outlaw to Burton's Bend.

'Hell, if he were in town . . . '. Morrison scratched his balding head. 'Just can't see it. I seen towns Barlow's passed through. They ain't alive no more. They just sort of wither like old flowers, as if the *hombre* gives off some sort of poison.'

'Inclined to agree with that. I've seen such myself. But after what happened in No See, well, he ain't used to bein' dogged; maybe that'll make him change his tactics. He ain't the smartest hardcase I've heard tell of, but he's sneaky as black hell and he ain't stayed alive this long with no sense of the game. If he's here, he's hidin' this time, waiting.'

'Waitin' for what?'

'Waiting for me. I saw it in his eyes, Ben. If I didn't come for him, he'd come for me. I'd rather it be on my terms.'

'Either way, I don't care much for the prospects. I think you finally bit off more than you can chew.'

'You might be right.' Duel sighed, then sucked in a deep breath. 'If he's here I have to find him.'

Ben Morrison leaned back in his chair, face going dark. 'I been debatin' tellin' you something, Duel. It didn't make much sense to me before but maybe with what you've told me it will now.'

'Tell me. Anything that'll give me an advantage with Barlow is what I'm looking for.'

'Well, I had a feeling I'd be seein' you right soon, let me tell you that. So when you walked into today I wasn't as surprised as I might have been.'

'No one knew I was headed this way, least in Burton's Bend.'

'That's true. But there was this gal askin' around about you. Asked the barkeep at the saloon, asked me, asked a number of folk. Reckon she probably got a good earful on you by the time she was through. You ain't exactly unknown here; might even say you're sort of a hero after bringing down Butch Cayton and folks do like to jaw 'bout their heroes.'

Duel leaned forward, sitting on the edge of his chair. A chill swept along his spine and his brow creased.

'What girl?'

'She looked like a bargirl to me. I think she even spent a bit of time last night at Burton's Saloon, workin' customers. She ain't been here long, maybe since yesterday afternoon, but she works fast. Didn't think much of it till now.'

'What she look like?' Duel tensed, knowing the description that would follow.

'Blonde, hard-looking but attractive.'

'Sounds like the girl Barlow escaped with. Reckon that clinches it: she's with him.'

'Could be he just released her and she was curious 'bout you.'

'Ain't likely. Barlow ain't left a trail of living victims and I 'spect if she weren't with him we'da found her sleeping with the buzzards along the trail somewhere.'

Morrison nodded. 'Reckon you're right.'

'She still in town?'

'Was last night. 'Less she rode out bright and early this mornin', she's here somewhere.'

'And if she's here, she's my lead to Barlow.'

Duel stood, drawing his shoulders back. He slid his Peacemaker in and out of his holster, getting the feel. A surge of adrenalin shot through his veins and his heart thudded mildly. 'Reckon I have a job to finish, then.'

Morrison stood, coming around the desk. 'I'll go with you. Two's got a better chance than one.'

'No!' Duel's voice came sharp as a whip crack. 'Barlow belongs to me after yesterday. Ain't no point in both of us risking our lives.'

'Look, Duel, I'm the marshal here — '

'Please, Ben, I'm askin' you as a friend. Leave him to me.' Their eyes met and Morrison's narrowed, a regretful look welding on to his face.

'I'm gettin' the feelin' I'm lettin' you go to your death.'

'Would have thought you'd have more faith in me by now, Ben. I'm crushed.' Duel tried to smile, but the expression came strained and fake.

'I do, son. But I've got faith in the

odds, too, and sooner or later we all lose. You ain't lost yet and I'm worried this will be your first time — and last.'

'You're wrong there, Ben. I've lost a lot of times. I left part of me scattered over a hundred trails and another part of me with a woman who didn't deserve the life she got. This is my chance to win it back.'

3

Duel Winston made his way along the boardwalk, heading towards Burton's Saloon. He felt sure now the girl was involved with Barlow, and where she was Barlow could not be far behind.

Duel had figured right: Barlow had changed his tactics in an effort to keep him off guard, but Duel had studied his craft of hunting men the way a master chess player studies the strategy of the board. He anticipated moves, and dulled edge or no, that skill served him good stead now. All he had to do was find the girl. Burton's Saloon was the logical place to start, for while John Barlow was a master player as well, likely his pawn was not. She was the weak link in Barlow's plan. That was the chance, the edge Duel needed.

He hoped.

He pushed through the batwing

doors into the saloon, eyes photographing every corner and cranny and sealing it in his memory. A thick haze of Durham smoke clouded the air. The sour reek of liquor and stale vomit assailed his nostrils. A clamor of voices and shaken dice rose from men seated at green-felted tables, playing chuck-a-luck or poker, some bucking the tiger. A piano player banged away discordantly on a honkytonk. Bargirls — the finest in New Mex, Burton always boasted — mingled, seeking to separate men from their wallets.

He spotted no sign of the girl and felt his hopes plunge. The overpowering notion Barlow was planning something, orchestrating his revenge, took Duel and he knew he had to strike fast to avoid it. But had Barlow and the girl already moved on, gone forward with whatever plan they had in mind. The girl had asked around about Duel for a reason and nearly everything about him was common knowledge, especially since that damn dime-novel writer had written up the story and for once gotten the facts right.

He threaded his way through the tables, sawdust grinding beneath his boots, and took a stool at the counter. The barkeep had his back to him, setting bottles into a hutch. The man turned, surprise lighting his face.

'Good lawdy almighty!' the fellow blurted. 'I've done seen a spook and lived to tell it!' The 'keep slapped a hand on the counter and bellowed a laugh. A large man, muscular, with a lean face and spectacles, dirty-blond hair resting on his shoulders.

'Been a long time, Dave.' Duel kept his voice low.

Dave Burton grinned. 'Never really expected to see you again, you know that? You still lookin' to meet a lady or that one in Whitehead Pass got you hog-tied?'

'Not yet, but she will if I have my way.'

'Pshaw! You'll never settle down, Duel. The trail's in your blood.'

Duel shrugged. 'Trail's flowing out of my blood. Bones get weary after so much ridin'. I plan to call it quits soon as I tie up a couple loose ends.' He reached into his pocket and pulled out the dodger, unfolding it.

Burton let out a prolonged sigh, face dropping expression. 'Aw, Gawd, Duel, that's a hell of a loose end.'

'You seen him?'

'If I had I'd be movin' to another town.'

'Maybe you've seen a friend of his?'

Burton cocked an eyebrow. 'Yeah?'

'Bargirl, blonde, woulda been askin' questions about me.'

An expression came back to the 'keep's face, a dark one. 'Aw, no! She was in last night. Called herself Delaney or something like that. Asked about you and if she could work for me during the evening. Saw her pumping my customers about you, but never went with one.'

'I figured as much.'

'She knows all this town knows about you, Duel. That ain't good, I reckon. If I'da knowed she was with John Barlow . . . .'

'Ain't your fault, Dave. Barlow's damn sneaky and likely made himself scarce while she did his dirty work.'

'Damn right. Nobody's seen hide nor hair of him or it'd be all over the place by now.' Burton's eyes suddenly shifted upward and his lips drew tight.

'What is it?' asked Duel, catching the expression. A cold tingling wave washed over him, warning him danger was close.

'That her?' Burton's voice dropped to a whisper, as he nudged his head towards the back of the room. Duel twisted on the stool to see a girl standing near the top of the stairs. She started down, hesitated, as if making sure it was safe.

His belly tightened. 'It's her.' And where the girl was . . .

He eased off the stool, drawing his Peacemaker and manoeuvring his way through the tables.

The girl froze, spotting him coming

towards her. Her eyes widened and he picked up his pace.

She whirled, dashing back up the stairs as he reached the bottom. She vanished around the corner as he started up.

He took the flight in a series of bounds, heart pounding, nerves freezing. Neither the girl nor Barlow had expected him to trail them so fast; that was obvious. If Duel had waited another few hours, likely they would have moved on, putting into motion whatever plan Barlow had devised. It was sheer luck that gave Duel the chance he had now.

He reached the top of the stairs, halting and pressing close to the wall. He peered around the corner, Peacemaker ready.

A short hallway, lit by a low-turned lantern, led to a series of rooms and cubicles.

A door banged shut at the end of the hall.

Duel moved forward, keeping the

Peacemaker close to his chest. Reaching the door he stopped, listened. No sound. She was in there, had to be, and he would force her to tell him about Barlow, but only if he could take her alive.

His hand edged out, clamping around the glass doorknob and twisting. With a deep breath he sent the door swinging inward, staying well out of the way of a possible shot.

Silence: except for his heart hammering like a muffled freight train and the throbbing of his pulse in his ears.

He edged around the corner, stopping just inside the door. The girl sat on the edge of the bed, a frightened look on her hard face.

Duel swung the Peacemaker towards her and took a step forward. 'Where is he?' His voice came low, threatening. He didn't really expect her to tell him right away but she would eventually.

She smiled, an expression that struck him as terribly out of place. His gaze narrowed, suspicion lighting in his eyes.

That trail-honed sense of wrongness probably saved his life then. With instant realization and reflex he knew he no longer had to look for John Barlow. John Barlow was here!

Duel jerked sideways as the thought flashed in his mind. A gun glanced from the top of his head, sending splinters of pain through his skull. The world jumped, slamming back into place and wetness streaked down his face.

Blood! His blood! The gun butt had opened a slash above his temple. He instinctively shot an arm up, to ward off a follow-up blow.

He felt the blow coming more than saw it. The Starr flashed past his shielding arm. Barlow tried to correct the descent, but couldn't in time.

It occurred to Duel both men had gotten a surprise. Barlow had not expected Duel this soon and Duel had not expected Barlow to be in the room: that put them on roughly even terms, though the hardcase had received a split second more warning. Barlow had grabbed the advantage and now Duel had to return the favor.

He swung a fist, aiming at the blurred target before him. Blood streamed into his eyes, painting the room crimson. His fist collided with the outlaw's jaw and the Starr flew from Barlow's grip. It skidded across the floor and Barlow roared.

The outlaw snapped a bootheel into Duel's ribs in return and Duel lost his own gun. A burst of nausea surged in his gut, but he had no time to worry about it. He swung again, this time missing.

Barlow charged him, slamming into his body and propelling him out into the hall. They went forward, towards the top of the stairs. Duel fought to regain his balance and vision, swiping at his eyes with a sleeve. Barlow sought to brain him with a hammering fist.

Duel avoided the blow, jerked a knee into Barlow's groin. The hardcase bellowed and froze.

Duel grabbed the advantage. He shot

a fist towards Barlow's head, hoping to hit something, anything, and the result satisfied him.

The outlaw stumbled backwards, Duel instantly leaping after him. They tangled, Duel discovering just how powerful the man was, despite his weakened condition at the moment.

Barlow heaved, lifting Duel clean off the floor, but Duel kicked, raking a bootheel across the hardcase's shin. Another roar burst from the outlaw's lips and both men went backwards.

Duel misjudged how close the stairs were. His foot slipped off the top step as it sought for a landing when Barlow let him go. Barlow came down atop him.

Duel twisted in a desperate attempt to right himself, but both men thudded down the stairs in a tumble.

Duel hit bottom, amazed nothing was broken. He gasped a breath, unable to locate John Barlow for the moment. He swiped blood and sweat from his vision and saw the outlaw, who had taken the brunt of the fall, pushing himself from the floor a few feet away.

Duel steadied himself and charged, ignoring the ringing pain in his body, intent on kicking Barlow in the face before the man got the chance to fight back.

Barlow moved faster than Duel would have thought possible. The kick sailed by Barlow's face and the hardcase caught Duel's leg, heaving, flipping Duel on to his back with a jarring thud.

Breath exploded from his lungs and his eyes roved in stunned sweeps across the ceiling. A low throbbing issued somewhere in his head, but he forced it away, knowing Barlow would be on him in a second and that would be the end of it. He struggled to move, push away the cobwebs in his brain.

Not in time.

Barlow landed atop him. Duel tried to roll out of the way, but was only partially successful.

Barlow, planting his feet, grabbed handfuls of Duel's shirt and tried to hoist him up as he straightened. Duel lashed out with a fist, ricocheting it from the outlaw's temple. Barlow staggered backwards.

Poker chips clattered across the floor as Barlow slammed into a table. Cards flew in all directions.

Duel sprang forward, but Barlow regained his balance and planted a boot in Duel's belly. An *omph!* burst from Duel's lips and nausea swelled in his gut. Giving it no thought, he lunged before Barlow had the chance to set for another blow. A clean shot would take Duel out of the game and he was determined not to let that happen.

He swung. Missed.

Barlow laughed, cocking a fist.

'*Don't!*' a voice snapped from behind them.

Through hazy vision Duel saw Ben Morrison had entered the bar, had a Peacemaker leveled on Barlow. Behind the counter, Dave Burton had grabbed a scattergun and was bringing it to aim on Barlow.

Barlow sneered, cursing. He leaped at Duel, despite the threat.

Duel was ready for it this time. He saw the look flash across the man's colorless eyes. No surrender, no alternate plan in case something went wrong. He would fight to the death.

Duel delivered a vicious uppercut. His gloved fist clacked Barlow's teeth together and snapped his head back. Barlow staggered in his step, eyes rolling upward. Duel swung again, not letting him recover.

John Barlow hit the floor with a heavy thump in a cloud of sawdust. He groaned, but didn't move. It was over. Barlow was defeated and Duel had lived to tell of it. He felt relief swell, but it was short-lived. He turned, staggering back towards the steps and up. He still had the girl to deal with. He went down the hall in cautious steps, stopping at the door and peering in.

The room was empty. An open window told him all he needed to know. He went to it, peered down, seeing an alleyway, but nothing else. She had escaped but he reckoned it didn't matter much. Girl like that would be lost without Barlow; she'd turn up in some saloon sooner or later, and when she did the law would have her.

He searched the floor, finding his own gun but noting the Starr was missing.

Going downstairs, he saw the marshal had already taken Barlow out. Dave Burton stared at Duel, shaking his head.

'Hell, he was right here in my saloon all the time an' I didn't even know it!'

'You're luckier for it, Dave. You'da known you'd be buried.'

Dave nodded and Duel walked towards the door, aching, nauseated, yet unburdened in spirit. The blood had stopped flowing from the gash on his head and he gained strength with each step as he walked the length of the boardwalk. An end. That what it was. An end to more than one thing. Barlow was behind bars and would be hanged for his crimes. Duel reckoned that day would come none too soon.

You made it out of this one . . .

Yes, he had. And after a brief stop he'd go back to her, if she'd have him. He almost smiled.

Reaching the marshal's office, he stepped in. Ben Morrison was sitting behind his desk, mopping sweat from his brow and looking relieved.

'Lord Almighty, Duel. I shoulda given you more credit. You got Barlow when I thought no man would.'

Duel shook his head, mopping a stream of sweat and moistened blood from his face with his bandanna. 'You hadn't distracted him he might have finished me, Ben. We both deserve the credit.'

John Barlow poised on the edge of a cot in the cell and Duel's gaze swung towards him.

'Nothing personal, Barlow,' Duel said flippantly. 'Just doing my job.'

Barlow sneered, colorless eyes narrowing. 'Hell it ain't. Let me tell you somethin', Mister Bounty Man. It is personal, now. Has been since yesterday. I'll git even no matter how long it takes.'

'Only thing you'll get is hanged,' Morrison put in. 'Got a rope with your name on it. You'll be dancin' at the end of it come dawn.'

'Give my regards to the Devil,' said Duel.

John Barlow spat on the floor.

Duel turned from him, looking at Morrison. 'Thanks, Ben. I mean it.' Duel shoved out his hand and the marshal shook it firmly.

'Hell, I should be thankin' you. Look at the recognition we're gonna get in Burton's Bend. I see lots of money flowin' into this town!'

'Deservedly so.' Duel finished mopping his face.

'Best get that tended to.'

'I will. Gonna stop at the doc's and get cleaned up.'

'After?' Morrison looked hopeful.

'After, I make a stop in a town east of

here and pick up my last customer.'

'Duel . . . ' Morrison dragged out the name.

'Don't worry. This one is easy. Simple case of wife stealin'. No killers involved.'

'Next time I hear from you it better be by wedding invite or you'll have me to answer to!'

Duel smiled, feeling better than he had in ages. 'You'll be first on the list . . . '.

4

The past was drawing to an end. A sense of freedom and peace swelled over Duel as he neared the town that would furnish his last bounty. This one would be easy, he assured himself. A simple case of tracking down an adulterer. Duel never usually paid no mind to moral offenders, but a certain mayor had offered him a bundle of money to fetch a fellow dubbed 'St Elmo', a kissing bandit of sorts. From the talk, Elmo was anything but dangerous — unless the fellow was left unattended with a body's wife. A smallish man, according to the dodger, with a peculiar penchant for garbing himself in black with a white collar to gain the trust of unsuspecting women, going so far as to even preach sermons at church on Sunday. An odd contradiction as Duel saw it. He also saw a certain dark humor to the whole affair, pardon the expression. Of course, it hadn't been his wife St Elmo had given alms to.

Duel had received word through a number of his usual sources St Elmo had high-tailed it to the small New Mex town of Peccadillo, pulling stakes in a flurry after being caught with his britches down by the mayor who hired Duel. A shotgun spitting both barrels had hastened the philandering bandit's departure. Fortunately, for St Elmo at any rate, the buckshot had missed — mostly. Rumor had it Elmo would be uncomfortable in a saddle for a spell.

Duel chuckled at the thought, mood uncharacteristically light. He felt as if a burden had been lifted from his soul now that Barlow was safely tucked away in Morrison's jail, sentenced to a necktie party the next morning by a one-man jury — the marshal. Duel would be only too happy to hear word of the outlaw's death, as would countless other folks and towns. With St

Elmo in hand, that would leave him only a journey to Wyoming to fetch his bounties.

Wyoming would be a right nice place to settle, he reckoned. She would like it there, far away from the life she led. He would like it. He had saved enough money, now, and with the bounties from Barlow and Elmo they could live comfortably for quite a spell. He had always dreamed of owning a small cattle spread, working the land, rooting in one spot. It was alien to him, a longing, overpowered far too long by the life he had led, his unsettled soul. But now . . . now things would be different. Sam would be with him and that's all he had ever wanted.

Wasn't it?

If that's so, why did you bother risking it all by chasing down Barlow? Why did you leave her at all?

The questions buffaloed him, he had to admit, but he supposed he had little need to dwell on them further. With Barlow's death Duel's wandering days would perish as well.

He wondered what she would think of the idea, being a rancher's wife. If not that, well, he could think of plenty of other dreams to hang a hat on. She hated what she was doing, living the life of a bar dove, a woman borrowed for a few dollars a night by drunken cowhands and ruffians; he knew that. He had asked her to give it up and she had promised she would — if he stayed with her. She was chained to her life as much as he was to his and each needed that one reason to escape those shackles. He was her reason, but, at the time, he had failed to see she was his. He felt something out there, out on the open trail, waiting for him always. Thought he had felt it. Barlow? Perhaps. But even Barlow's capture and death couldn't fill the longing space inside him. Only one thing could.

Her face rose in his mind and he smiled, savoring the vision. 'I've missed you . . . '. The words drifted over the desert. He hoped she had missed him as well, and had waited.

The desert fell away after another hour, melding into sloping valleys and low hills. Beyond would be the grassy plains and cattle-grazing lands of the Pecos River.

Peccadillo appeared in the distance. A small town, it flanked the outskirts of the huge cattle empires occupying the Pecos Valley. A town rife with cathouses, gambling dens, and every concoction a weary cowhand could possibly find intoxicating after a hard day tending herd. Like many such towns in the area, it boasted rough and rowdy pleasures and a decided lack of decent law.

He rode into town, gaze studying the busy streets as the noon sun glittered from dusty windows and sparkled from troughs. He noticed more saloons than shops, five or more to either side. Finding this Elmo character might prove harder than he thought. The man demonstrated an attachment to women and he'd have no trouble finding them in the saloons of Peccadillo.

Duel drew up in front of the marshal's office. Might as well start there. He vowed not to waste a whole lot of time collaring St Elmo. If he found him quickly he'd haul the fellow up to Burton's Bend and deposit him in Morrison's jail for safe keeping until he returned to Wyoming. If not, well, he reckoned it mattered little. He would ride to Whitehead Pass and start his — *their* — new life.

* * *

'You best let me outa here, Marshal.' John Barlow perched on the edge of the cot, head lifted, pale eyes locked on Ben Morrison, who sat behind his desk eating lunch. Those eyes, hollow things, unnerved him, boogered him. The hardcase was as empty inside as any man he'd ever laid eyes on. No compassion, no remorse, no humanity lived behind those colorless orbs. Emptiness; that's all Morrison saw.

Complete, utter emptiness. Like God had forgotten to fill the bastard up with whatever makes a body human when he was born.

Morrison cursed the men for not finishing construction of the gallows in time for the hanging this morning. They had promised by dusk, but gallows had never been needed in Burton's Bend 'fore now. Morrison kept a tight hand on criminal activity; he usually dealt with any problems with lead, and that was seldom. Barlow was a horse of a different color, a horse with no color, make that. Morrison would have preferred shooting the hardcase but the town wanted to make a spectacle of it. Not often were men of Barlow's infamy corraled, and his hanging would be done up with all the trimmings. The local papers had geared up to cover it, hiring an artist to capture every nuance of Barlow's expression when the distance between his chin and his shoulders suddenly got three inches farther apart, courtesy of a hemp necktie. Morrison didn't care for it a lick. The longer Barlow remained alive the more possibility a mistake would be made. Duel wouldn't have liked it either; only reason the bounty hunter hadn't stuck around was because he trusted Morrison to get the job done at dawn.

'Hope I didn't let you down, son . . . ' he muttered, feeling a knot of tension grow in his belly.

'Talkin' to yourself, now, Marshal?' Barlow laughed. 'I have that effect on folks, you know. Folks are just plain scared of me.'

'I ain't scared of you, Barlow. Ain't scared of no man.'

'That so? We'll see.'

Morrison's face pinched. He glanced at his plate of beans, suddenly devoid of appetite. 'What do you mean by that?'

'I mean you ain't never gonna get me to those gallows. Waste of time buildin' them. An' you know I ain't one for idle threats. I'll see you dead 'fore that happens.'

'Come sundown you'll be dancin' at the end of that rope way you deserve. You shoulda been 'fore now.'

'You wouldn'ta hung me this mornin', neither. If you'da tried . . . ' Barlow's eyes narrowed.

'I should just fill you fulla lead and be done with it.' Morrison felt vaguely worried for a reason he couldn't figure. John Barlow was safely in that cell, unarmed, yet somehow the hardcase intimidated him, as if he possessed some force that reached out and took hold of your courage, throttled it.

'Your friend, Winston, I know all about him . . . I'll kill him after I kill you. Not the same way though. I'll do him right slow, after I find what means most to him and make him suffer with it.'

Morrison suppressed the urge to shudder. The hardcase said it with too much confidence, too much surety, and that bothered him. Most outlaws became desperate when the hour of their death closed in. They said things, sure, but usually it amounted to begging or blasphemy. Barlow was too calm, too meaningful in his talk.

Morrison pushed away his plate. 'Duel Winston's got no ties nowhere, Barlow. 'Sides, it don't matter 'cause you won't get the chance. I'll see to that myself.'

Barlow laughed and Morrison wanted to shudder again. 'He's got ties, lawman. I saw it in his eyes. He's got the look of a man waitin' to get out and after that it's all over but the butcherin'. I know everything about him and I know what — *who* — he's lookin' for. Hear she's right pretty, too.'

Morrison stiffened. Barlow *did* know, somehow. He had found out about Sam, the attachment Duel had to her. '*The look of a man waitin' to get out*': Barlow was right about that, too. Morrison had glimpsed the same thing in Winston's eyes, a burning need to put an end to one phase of his life and move onto the one he was meant for. That's how Morrison knew Duel would keep his word when he retrieved his last quarry. He knew Duel would return to a woman in a small town a short piece from the Pecos and Ben would be best man at a wedding. He had reckoned Duel's past was ready for buryin' but a swelling dread told him Duel would run into difficulties he hadn't counted on.

Morrison fought off the sudden urge to draw his Peacemaker and put an extra eye in Barlow's forehead. He wanted to, God, he wanted to. Waiting around for the hangin' was too much on his raw nerves. The outlaw's jawin' didn't help the situation, either.

Little held him back from killing the hardcase, except the code he'd always held to that he wouldn't shoot a man who wasn't threatening him directly and at the moment Barlow appeared to be little threat. He would be hanged at dusk and that would be that. A grisly chapter in the West would come to a close; Ben Morrison and Duel Winston would go on with their lives and John Barlow would pass into legend.

‘Why don’t you just shut the hell up!’ Morrison snapped.

Barlow smirked. ‘What’s the matter, Marshal? You look a mite pale to me.’ Barlow’s soulless glare intensified. ‘Let me out, Morrison. This is the last time I’m askin’.’

‘I’ll spit on your grave; that’s the most courtesy you’ll get from me.’

‘Too bad. Now you’re a dead man, Marshal. ’Course, I ain’t a man of my word, anyhow, so I reckon it didn’t matter.’

The door burst open and Morrison started. Coming half out of his seat, he froze, hands on the desk top.

‘Uh-uh, honeybun.’ A blonde girl leveled a Starr .36 at his chest. ‘Wouldn’t wanna have ta shoot y’all, now.’

‘You . . . ’. Morrison recognized the girl who’d been asking around about Duel Winston. He thought she had fled by now, but had his deputies out searching the town for her just in case. He, Duel as well, had misjudged the dove's loyalty to Barlow. With a sudden pooling of ice in his belly he knew the reason for Barlow's cockiness: she had been his ace all along.

Barlow let out a high-pitched cackle and stood, coming close to the bars.

'You awraht, Johnny?' Delaney asked, keeping her sights on the marshal.

'Reckon I'm right fine, now.' He nodded at the marshal. 'Kill him!'

Morrison's heart beat in his throat. His gaze swung from Barlow to the girl.

The girl hesitated, hand quivering. Her eyes widened. 'You know I cain't kill nobody, Johnny. You' — she nudged the Starr at the marshal — 'drop your gunbelt, real slowlahk.'

Morrison struggled to gauge the dove. She said she couldn't kill. Perhaps not in cold blood, but something told him if he went for his gun she would come by the nerve.

'That's right, lawman,' Barlow said, picking up on the marshal's thoughts. 'She will pull that trigger if you try anything.'

'I'm dead anyway . . . ' Morrison said, in a somber tone and Barlow acquired a gleam of worry in his pale eyes.

Morrison moved, spinning around the desk while the girl had her attention on Barlow. He intended to take her before she could react, wrest the Starr from his grip. He didn't make it.

She uttered a gasp and the Starr swung towards him. Her finger jerked the trigger without much aim. The piece blasted, report reverberating in the small office like caged thunder.

Morrison jolted in his tracks, gaze dropping to the crimson starburst swelling across his gut. His hands gripped at the wounds in a desperate attempt to staunch the flow of blood, but crimson streamed between his fingers. His legs flooded with weakness. His mouth dropped open and he crumpled to the floor.

The dove stared, eyes wide, a horrified expression on her face. 'Gawdammit, Johnny! I didn't wanna kill nobody!'

Barlow laughed. 'Sometimes you gotta butcher the hog to make bacon.'

'He ain't no hawg, Johnny. He's a man.'

Barlow grunted. 'Sometimes you're plumb stupid, Delaney, you know that?'

'Don't talk ta me lahk that, Johnny. You know I don't lahk it.'

'I'll talk to you any goddamned way I want and you'll lap it up.' She stared at him and his eyes seemed to swallow her will. 'Now get me those keys.'

The blonde glanced at the sprawled form of Morrison, jerked her gaze away, then went to the keyring hanging from a nail behind the marshal's desk.

Unlocking the cell door, she handed Barlow the Starr. Barlow went to the desk and located his gunbelt and knife in a drawer, strapping them on.

'I done good, huh, Johnny?' Delaney looked hopeful.

'Yeah, you done real good.' He lashed out in a sharp arc, callused knuckles ricocheting from her jaw. She bleated, falling to the floor. Tears streamed down her cheeks and she wiped blood from her lips.

'Don't you ever talk back to me again, woman. You got that?'

She looked up, eyes pleading. 'I won't no more, Johnny, I swear I won't.'

'Get up.'

She pushed herself to her feet, shaky. Barlow stepped over to the marshal, who lay unmoving. A moan escaped Morrison's lips.

'Looks like I was right, don't it, Marshal?' Barlow buried a boot toe in Morrison's ribs. The marshal groaned and his hands twitched.

'We best be takin' ourselves from here, Johnny.' A worried expression crossed Delaney's features. 'Someone's gonna hear that shot.'

Barlow cocked an eyebrow. 'So? Ain't no one foolhardy enough to try an' stop us, 'cept that bounty man and I got it all worked out for him.'

'Cain't we just go somewhere, Johnny, and ferget all this? Please, Johnny? You promised we would.'

‘Well, sometimes I ain’t so partial to the truth, am I, now?’ His pale eyes drilled her and she cowered, as if expecting another blow. She touched her swelling lip, wiping a speck of blood away. He grabbed her arm. ‘C’mon, we got a passenger to pick up ’fore headin’ back home.’

‘Home?’

‘Home.’

* * *

St Elmo proved easier to locate than Duel expected. It seemed a man pretending to be a preacher had come into Peccadillo a spell ago and remained, finding a haven of unclaimed souls to save.

Duel bet they were female souls.

The marshal, a lawman of little better caliber than the one he’d encountered in No See, informed him St Elmo could be found nightly at the .45 Caliber Saloon, espousing the benefits of a holy life, one he could lead select ladies to if only they spent a few hours listening to the 'word'. Duel bet religion had little to do with the kind of sermon St Elmo was partial to.

He pushed through the batwings as dusk swept through Peccadillo, painting shadows across the streets and touching the air with a chill. The saloon, like a hundred others scattered across the south-west, was crowded with cow-hands. The atmosphere ripped with the bellow of laughter and shouts, and a honky-tonk sorely in need of tuning. He peered through the thick tobacco haze in search of the fellow decorating his Wanted dodger. St Elmo was nowhere to be seen. He had expected the man to be spouting one of his nightly sermons, but maybe the job wouldn't prove that easy. He checked his Peacemaker, doubting he'd have to use it but opting to take no chances.

Making his way to the counter, he slapped a silver dollar on the bar, then pulled out a second.

'The first is for the whiskey,' Duel

said and the 'keep poured the drink.

'Somethin' else you're lookin' for, mister? Maybe a lady?'

'I'm looking for a man.' Duel slid the silver dollar across the counter. The 'keep's face took a peculiar expression and Duel chuckled. He pulled the Wanted dodger from his pocket and tossed it down. 'This man.' He tapped the poster.

'Hey, that's St Elmo!' the 'keep blurted.

'You've seen him?' Duel cocked an eyebrow.

'Hell, yeah, I seen him! Was here just a few minutes ago. Comes in ever' night. But he's a right upstandin' fella. Always helps those in need . . . ' The 'keep let the words trail off and Duel caught his meaning. Translation: he spent money on women and the 'keep collected a goodly percentage.

'I reckon he does.' Duel folded the dodger and tucked it away.

'You a bounty hunter?'

'Not for much longer. Soon as I find

Elmo, I'm retired.'

'What's he done?'

Duel shrugged. He reckoned it wouldn't hurt to tell. 'Took something that didn't belong to him — mayor's wife.'

'Reckon I don't know where he went.' The 'keep's face suddenly tightened. Duel could tell the man was thinking of lost revenue. He bet Elmo had been good for business, if the good looks of the doves in the place served any indication.

Duel dug into a pocket and plucked out two double eagles, letting them clink on the counter top. The 'keep's eyes widened and his expression softened.

'This help your memory?'

'Upstairs with Tally, one of my girls . . . giving her a sermon.'

'I imagine.' Duel pushed the coins closer and the 'keep snatched them up, greed glinting in his eyes. He walked away with a smile.

Duel swigged the whiskey and

thunked the glass down, smiling. St Elmo was due for a sermon of a different sort, Duel figured. If the mayor's anger was any indication, the amorous bandit stood to end up at the hard end of another kind of gospel — one that involved a particular commandment about wife stealing.

Duel stood and threaded his way through the tables, heading to the stairs at the back of the room. He went up, going down a long hallway papered with a red flower pattern and lit by a single low-turned lantern. It reminded him of countless other such hallways. Dingy and unattractive, designed to make the doves look more appealing. Doors to either side were open, except for one in the middle. That would be St Elmo. He padded up to it, easing the Peacemaker from its holster. While he expected no problem, he refused to get complacent on his last case. Cornered men sometimes did peculiar things.

Gripping the doorhandle, he turned it, easing the door open. Stepping into the room, he leveled his gun on two persons in a bed.

A dark-haired girl gasped, jerking bedcovers over her bosom.

'Who are you?' the man next to her demanded in a voice higher than any man should have. The fellow looked younger than the dodger made him out to be, handsome in a genteel way. He was smallish with pomaded black hair, a sharp nose, and eyes that seemed to always look anywhere but straight at you. He carried an innocent, almost angelic expression. Duel could see how he could buffalo unsuspecting women, though the woman next to him was likely the one doing the conning in this case.

Duel's gaze swept the drab room, the bed and a nightstand holding a lantern the only furniture. A threadbare carpet, grimy and wholly unappealing, lay at the foot of the bed.

'Name's Duel Winston. I came to collect you for Mayor Tidly.'

The man's eyes widened and the

angelic expression dropped from his face, replaced by one of fear. 'No, please, I can't go back there! I'll pay you anything!'

'Doubt you could match what the mayor's payin' me and I 'spect it's about time you answered for your crimes.'

'I didn't do nothin'!'

'Way I heard it, you stole the mayor's wife.'

'Didn't steal her! Just borrowed her a spell.'

'Mayor don't see it that way.'

Elmo scowled. ''Spose there ain't no talkin' about this?'

'Get dressed.'

Elmo complied. He slid out of bed and pulled on his trousers and shirt, both black, Duel noted. He tucked a white collar into a pocket and Duel chuckled inwardly. The girl eyed the proceedings with little interest.

'Reckon this means I don't get paid.' She sneered, obviously holding little worry over what would happen to Elmo.

Duel took a couple of bills from his pocket and tossed them on the bed. 'Make a donation to church Sunday morning.'

'Thanks, gent!' The girl beamed, snapping up the notes.

'You ready?' Duel asked, glancing at Elmo.

Elmo's lips tightened, but he nodded.

Duel guided him out of the saloon. He had hitched two horses, his own and a sorrel he'd acquired from the livery, to the rail in front of the saloon. He holstered his gun, now sure Elmo wasn't the type to resist.

'Can you ride, or is your rump too sore?'

'Do I have a choice?'

'I could throw you across the saddle and you can take the trip on your belly.'

'I can ride.'

'Up.' Duel nudged his head to the sorrel and mounted. Elmo frowned and stepped into the saddle.

Duel nodded to the end of town and they set the horses into a trot.

'Where are we going?' St Elmo asked in his too-high voice.

'Town called Burton's Bend. Gonna leave you with a friend of mine for safe keeping while I tend to a bit of business I've left too long unfinished.'

'He'll kill me, you know. The mayor, I mean. He's right annoyed he caught me with his wife.'

'So I hear.'

'My death will be on your hands, sir, yes, it will.'

'I reckon I can live with that.' Duel said it with humor but wondered if what the man were saying was true. He would talk to the mayor and get his word nothing untoward would happen to St Elmo. The man deserved punishment but more along the lines of getting the devil scared out of him, so to speak. He didn't deserve hanging and Duel would not be happy if that were what the mayor had in mind.

'Sir, I plead to your mercy. The wife of the mayor was tired of being ignored. I just gave her what she couldn't get from her husband, a little love and attention. He'd do best to get his own house in order 'stead of chasin' after the likes of me.'

'Maybe you're right, but it don't change the fact that you took advantage of the situation, not to mention makin' a mockery of the Lord.'

'Are you a religious man, sir?' A gleam of hope appeared in St Elmo's eyes.

'Don't get your hopes up, Elmo. It won't work.'

'Then why not tell me?'

Duel shrugged. 'Reckon I'm not your Sunday churchgoer, but I believe somethin's guidin' me, otherwise I wouldn't live long in my line of work. Ain't much for your type of preachin', but I ain't got no call to see it mocked by those who don't like it.'

'You believe I'm mocking it?'

'I do. Using the Lord's Word for . . . well, you get the idea.'

'I assure you, I believe every word of what I'm sayin', Mr Winston. I assure you I do. I'm a God-fearing man. Jest I got this problem with women — I like 'em. I like 'em too much.'

'Most of the time I wouldn't see that as a problem, Elmo. But when you go 'bout takin' other folks' wives . . . well, most menfolk I know would get right peeled about that.'

Elmo sighed, staring straight ahead into the night. They rode a bit farther and Duel reined up near a stream flanked by clusters of cottonwoods. It would be the last before the trail to Burton's Bend turned dusty and rocky, barren. They would make camp here for the night and head to the town with first light.

Duel dismounted, hobbling his bay and instructing Elmo to do the same. After hitching the horses to a cottonwood branch, Duel gathered loose twigs and started a fire. He foraged in his gear, pulling out an iron fry pan and a blue-speckled enameled coffee pot. Filling the pot with stream water and Arbuckle's beans, he set it aboiling.

With his bowie knife he carved bacon into the fry pan and set it sizzling. The smoky scent rose in the night and made his mouth water. Duel handed Elmo a hardtack biscuit then opened a can of beans and cooked them with the bacon. After devouring the beans, he sopped up the sauce and bacon grease with the biscuit. Elmo did the same.

The meal finished, Duel quickly scoured the pan in the stream while Elmo washed the plates.

Duel filled two tin cups with coffee, handing one to Elmo, then lowering himself on to the bedding he'd unrolled. He sipped the coffee, gazing out at the landscape, shady blue and alive with the sounds of the night. Stars glittered like ice chips in the velvet sky, twin reflections within the murmuring stream. The night would be cool, but the fire blazing between them would make it comfortable.

'You're searching for something, Mr Winston — Duel, if I may?' Elmo said, finishing his coffee.

Duel shrugged, glancing at him. 'Yeah?'

'Duel it is, then. Interesting name, yes, sir.'

Duel eyed the younger man. 'I can see where you'd get on folks' nerves.' He grunted and leaned back on the saddle he would make his pillow. He watched the stream flow, listening to the night creatures chattering. A sense of peace filtered over him, broken suddenly by Elmo's shrill voice.

'I can see it in your eyes, you know.'

'What's that?' Duel didn't particularly care for where the conversation was leading.

'You're missing something in your life. You got an empty place inside you.'

'I was right, you're damn annoying.'

Elmo laughed it off. 'You can deny it all you want, Mr — Duel. But it's there. You're sick of this line of work.'

'You always so good at reading folks?' Duel cast him an annoyed glare, wondering how the man had been so perceptive.

'Have to be. If I weren't, how you think a fella like me'd survive out here?'

'You got a point. 'Cept you're not quite right, Elmo.'

'No?'

'See, I aim to quit. You're my last bounty, then I'm gonna build me a cattle ranch up Wyoming way.'

Elmo cocked an eyebrow. 'Then why not let me go? You don't need me. You said you were quitting. Make a fresh start. It's your salvation, Duel Winston. Grab it by the horns and don't look back.'

Duel chuckled and gained his feet. 'You know, I reckon you're right.'

Elmo smiled beatifically.

Duel went to his gear and selected a rope, then went back to Elmo and doubled over him. 'Give me your hands.'

Elmo's expression dropped, but he held out his hands. Duel tied them then secured Elmo's feet.

Elmo frowned. 'What are you doing?'

'Making sure you don't run off on

me in the middle of the night.'

'Thought you said I was right?'

'You were . . . and I'll start right after I get you where you're going.' Duel laughed and dropped back on to his bedding, settling in and resting his head on the saddle.

Elmo squirmed, uncomfortable with the ropes, but it couldn't be helped. Elmo might not be the type to use force on Duel, but he was the type to high-tail it in the dead of night.

'Reckon there's snakes out here?' Elmo suddenly asked.

Duel chuckled. 'You see one wake me up . . . ' Duel set his hat over his eyes. He relaxed as much as a man like him could, focusing on the gurgle of the stream and the music of the night.

5

'I'm askin' you to give it up, Duel,' said Samantha Dale, emerald eyes pleading.

Duel struggled to avoid her stare, eyes searching every nook and cranny of the small room above the saloon. If he met her gaze his resolve might crumble and he'd be tempted to give in. He wasn't ready to quit the trail just yet, even with the last of the Cayton gang out of business. The wilderness had embedded itself into his soul, that hunger for unknown fate, roving. Yet confusion took him whenever she was near. Times aplenty he had considered just what she asked him to do — leave the rambling, force away that driven entity that possessed him, settle somewhere, anywhere as long as they did it together. He had little to show for all his years as a bounty hunter. Money earned disappeared like ice in the desert, in poker games, with empty whiskey bottles and women of questionable backgrounds and motives. If he quit now they'd be starting with nothing and he wouldn't have that. From this point, he would save his bounties; gambling and especially other women held precious little appeal to him now that he had met Sam.

Despite the stirrings of emotion he felt for her, despite the withering of the enraged man he had been, something stronger pulled him back. Something left undone, something unfulfilled by the endless nights spent sleeping under the stars, the days spent tracking outlaws. Hired gun, bounty hunter, manhunter, or just plain devil, call him what you would; he really didn't give a damn. It all stacked up the same way. He still didn't belong any one place yet, to any one life, until he confronted whatever fate held in store for him. What that was, well, he couldn't be sure, but he knew it would come soon and after that he'd be free to live.

Strange, these questions, these stirrings inside. He had felt them from the first moment he met her. Most men wouldn't have called her much, a bargirl in a cowtown a short piece from the Pecos. At first he might have been inclined to agree. Another woman in a string of forgotten names and frozen feelings.

She was different. She didn't belong to her life any more than he belonged to his. She had been caught by circumstance as had he, and good intentions aside, each had become what they had become: empty somewhere, but waiting, wanting. Funny, he felt that chance of being filled slipping away, compliments of his own pigheadedness. She knew it, too. She knew it and was reaching out to stop it.

He drew a deep breath, peering at her, seeing the tenseness on her face, a pretty face, though hard-edged. Her blonde hair, piled high with large loops, cork-screwing to either side of her coral-tinted cheeks, cascaded over her bare shoulders. Her peek-a-boo top accentuated her ample bosom, a ruffled skirt flared out from full hips. And eyes, eyes as green and crystal as the richest emeralds.

'I want to stay, Sam. Lord knows I want to.'

'Then do it,' she said, voice low, knowing.

'I can't . . . ' He turned away, going to the window and staring out into the inky night. He saw her reflection in the glass, the hurt plain on her face. He felt his resolve waver, almost said, 'I'll stay', but couldn't get the words out.

You're a fool, Duel Winston, you know that?

He turned from the window and went to her, pulling her into his arms. She buried her head in his shoulder.

'I have to leave. I have no choice.'

'I don't understand. You said you loved me and wanted me. You're the first man who ever treated me like I was something, made me feel like a lady. I never felt that before.'

'Reckon I never felt the things I'm feelin', either, but I ain't ready to build us a life. I got . . . things to finish. Somethin's out there callin' to me, tellin' me I won't be able to stay put till it's done. I ain't sure what it is, but it's there and I'll know it when I meet it, but not till then. Then I'll come back and we can start over some place.'

She pushed him away suddenly, anger darkening her face, narrowing her eyes and tightening her lips. 'You expect me to wait for ever, Duel Winston? You expect me to just wait around while you go out and chase your goddamn ghosts? I meet men a'plenty. I can have my pick of whatever one I fancy!' Tears flowed and she put her face in her hands.

Duel lowered his head, eyes closing, opening, emotion choking his throat. 'I know you can, Sam. I wouldn't blame you a lick if you didn't wait. You don't deserve a man who can't give you a definite answer and I reckon I don't deserve to have a woman as fine as yourself wait for me.'

Her face came out of her hands, tears smudging the kohl around her eyes, tracking black over her cheeks. 'A woman as fine as me?' The words came bitter, with an almost hysterical laugh of mockery. 'As fine as me? Look at me, Duel Winston! Look at me real close and tell me what you see?'

He looked, seeing through the make-up and tarnish. Words stumbled in his mind. 'I . . . see a woman who don't belong where she is. I see a woman who means more to me than anything ever has.'

'Then take me away from this . . . *place*. Take me away from the lonely nights, the beds that are always empty no matter how many men fill them. Take me away from all this misery, Duel. Prove to me what you're sayin'.'

He shook his head slowly, walking in weighted steps to the door, hesitating. 'I can't, Samantha. I wish to God I could, but I can't and I'm damned if I can tell you why.'

Her lips drew tight and the anger returned. 'You take a good look at me, Duel Winston! 'Cause when you finally realize what we got it might be too late. I'm a whore, Duel, and no matter what you see beneath that that's what the fact is. And that's the way I'll always be if you go.'

'You ain't that, Sam. Whatever you are, whatever you do, you ain't that.' He swallowed, tears swelling in his eyes; he forced them back and opened the door.

'I love you, Duel!' she yelled as he closed the door softly and stood in the hall a moment. The leaden emptiness inside made him want to turn around, give up the life he was wasting. He started down the hall, steps faltering, her name bittersweet on his lips and her tears etched into his heart.

* * *

Duel sat bolt upright, heart pounding with the emotion left over from the dream. The memory of leaving her cut through him with the sharpness of a sword. He forced his breathing to steady, drawing large gulps of cool night air.

'Bad dream?' asked Elmo, peering up at him.

Duel glanced over, searching for his voice. 'What the hell are you doing still awake?' he snapped, a bit embarrassed. He gazed at the sky, seeing the moon had jumped three hours' worth of distance across the diamond-studded velvet.

'Ain't particularly easy to sleep with your hands and legs all trussed up, now, is it?'

Duel shook his head. 'Reckon it ain't, but I ain't about to untie you.'

'I give you my word as a gentleman I won't run off.'

Duel almost laughed. 'Way I hear it you gave your word to the mayor, too. Weren't much of a gentleman there.'

'Was with his wife,' Elmo said sarcastically.

'Reckon you should be a little less

kindly then. It'd save you a bellyful of trouble.' Duel lay back, resting his head on the saddle and staring up at the stars. The magnificence of the heavens still awed him, relaxed him and he grew lost in thought. His mind drifted back to Sam and the dream. He'd left her a little over a year ago. He reckoned not many a night had passed that she hadn't come on his mind.

She called herself a whore, but he would never call her that, nor allow anyone else to. A victim; she was that. She wasn't like the rest of the doves. She had come into bad times, done what she had to do to survive. Her parents had been killed in an Apache raid and she had been taken captive by the Indians. But not for long. Rescued as the Apache met with multiple defeats at the hands of the cavalry, she'd been placed in a foster home. After that she had little chance. At home in neither world, white nor Indian, she ran off, a girl of fourteen or fifteen — and girls alone in the West found little chance of survival. She would have been better off left with the Apache, she had told Duel, though she despised them for what they had done to her parents. With time she had grown almost numb to that. They had treated her well, but she realized she had no life with them either.

A whore? Never in his eyes. A woman. A fine woman, with frailties and faults, no less and no more than he had himself. He'd give anything to turn back the year, have the decision to make again. The feeling that had called to him so strongly, told him of unfinished business, had smoldered in that time. He'd grown more and more discontent with the life he led, with all the death. Even John Barlow didn't really matter in the scheme of things. The outlaw just symbolized a finish he had put on the man he had been that night he turned her away.

'A woman?' Elmo suddenly broke the silence.

'What?' Duel came from his thoughts.

'I said, a woman. You were thinking about a woman.'

'How the hell you know that?' Duel's brow crinkled.

Elmo shrugged. 'Man like you, it's either a woman or outlaw and you said this was your last job so I figured it wasn't the outlaw.'

'You figured right.'

'Who is she?'

'Why you askin'?'

'Women's a specialty of mine, you might say.'

'Reckon they are, at that.' Duel drew in a long breath. 'Her name's Samantha Dale. She . . . works in a town not too far from here, Whitehead Pass. I'm going to see her after I drop you off in Burton's Bend.'

'She want to see you?'

'Sure hope to hell. She's been alone a spell, though.'

'If she loves you, she waited.'

'Hope you're right, Elmo.'

'Near always am when it comes to the fair sex.'

‘’Cept in the case of the mayor.’ Duel grinned.

‘We’re all entitled to a lapse in judgement.’

‘Sounds to me like you had yourself more than your share.’

Elmo looked at him. ‘Maybe you could say the same?’

Duel tensed, forced himself to relax. ‘Maybe I could.’

Elmo went silent and Duel drifted with his thoughts, unable to get back to sleep. After a half-hour he looked over to see Elmo still awake and propped himself on his elbows. ‘Reckon I won’t be sleeping the rest of the night. You?’

‘Not likely.’

Duel stood and rolled his bedding. ‘Might as well get to Burton’s Bend early in that case. Ain’t long till first light and it beats sittin’ here.’

‘Speak for yourself.’

Duel untied Elmo and the smaller man massaged his wrists. They saddled horses and collected gear, setting off in the direction of Burton’s Bend.

They rode in silence until Elmo gazed at Duel, who sat morose and stiff in his saddle.

'What makes a man like you?' Elmo asked.

Duel eyed him. 'What do you mean?'

'I mean a man who chases down other men, dangerous men. It ain't just the money, though for some it might be.'

'What makes you think I'm any different? Maybe it is for the money.'

'No, it ain't. I can tell. You're glad to be quittin'. Some fellas do it 'cause they enjoy it, huntin' a man; some do it 'cause they feel it's their duty — you've got that but there's more.'

'Yeah?' Duel felt his belly tighten.

'Yeah. The rest do it 'cause they have to. Somethin' eats at 'em inside, drives 'em to do it. That's what you got the most.'

Duel swallowed. Memories stirred in the depths of his mind. 'I mighta done it for justice's sake. Reckon I coulda quit sooner if that were all of it.'

'You mighta stayed with that gal.'

Duel nodded. 'I was a boy, maybe twelve or so, it's hard to recollect exactly. But I recollect the rest too clear. I was travelin' with my parents to Montana by stage. Some men, hard-cases in masks, robbed the stage. They killed my pa and the driver right off, but they did . . . *things* to my ma before they finally shot her. I watched her die . . . ' A tear slid down his cheek and he prayed Elmo didn't see it in the darkness. His voice broke. 'They kicked the hell outa me and rode off. I survived . . . sort of.'

'Sort of?' Elmo looked puzzled.

'A piece of me stayed in that time, I reckon. I wasn't right for a long spell after it happened. Then I got the idea I could make it right. I never saw their faces, those men, but every outlaw I bring down wears those masks.'

'Now it's different?'

Duel shrugged, getting control of himself. 'Now maybe it's time to let the past be . . . '

* * *

The saloon in Whitehead Pass had just closed. Samantha Dale finished wiping out glasses and setting them behind the counter. Scanning the bar-room, she made sure she had collected them all. She had become little more than a waitress, but she preferred it that way, thankful Ben let her do that instead of, well, most 'keeps weren't as tolerant with their doves. But the thought of drunken cowhands pawing at her revolted her now. Sour breath, bodies stinking of sweat and dung. She could never go back to the way she had lived before . . . *him*. Although she made far less money serving whiskey and sweet talk, she felt different about herself, somehow alive, though wanting. She could thank him for that at least.

She hadn't given up thinking about him, and in the empty hours after closing that feeling strengthened, burned inside. She kept wondering whether he would return, perhaps foolishly, whether he would keep his word. The other doves called her loco, waitin' on a man. Men like that always made promises to doves, maybe they even intended keeping them until the next town came along and another bargirl chased the promise from their heads. Duel wouldn't lose the wanderlust in his blood or he'd be killed, even if he did remember her.

It was just an old dream and for now it kept her going. She scolded herself for it, refusing to let hope take too big a hold on her. He's lost out there on the trail, in that life. As lost as she was in hers.

She shook her head, frowning, a choking sense of hopelessness rising in her bosom. She couldn't let herself think that. She had seen something different in Duel Winston, something that told her he was the first man she had ever met who kept his promises. But it had been so long . . .

She recollected the night he left, the hurt inside her, the emptiness. She recollected telling herself the hell with him! She would find someone better, someone who would take her away from this life and not be beholden to the wind. How could she compete with something like that?

Maybe he would find another woman. Someone better, proper, the way a lady should be. She wanted to be a lady, a fine lady, prim and proper, dressin' in fancy dresses and sippin' tea, oh how she wanted it. But things hadn't turned out that way and it was too late now, wasn't it?

Maybe. Duel had called her a lady, a fine woman. And by God she believed he meant it. He made her almost believe she was, something above the rest of the type in places like Ben's Saloon.

'You thinkin' 'bout that fella again?'

She came from her reverie and turned to see Ben staring at her, pulling a small comb through his neat beard. It wasn't the first time he'd caught her daydreaming.

'I keep hopin' . . . ' Her voice was almost a whisper.

'Can't live on hope, Sammy.'

Her emerald eyes narrowed. 'It's the only thing I can live on.' She smiled, but the expression was forced.

'You might have to if you don't get a move on and git this place lookin' respectable!' Ben's voice sounded harsh but she knew he was teasing her. The man had become almost a father to her, taking her in years ago. He had been responsible in a way for what she had become, but she couldn't blame him for it. She had made her mistakes. Ben was at heart a decent man; he protected the girls here.

She was about to give him a sarcastic answer when the batwings suddenly parted. She looked over to see a man and woman step into the saloon. An instant chill skittered along her spine as her emerald eyes met the colorless gaze of the man. Her mouth parted slightly. She saw nothing in those eyes, nothing but emptiness and frozen spaces. A winter of a man, cold and unforgiving. She searched the rest of his features, the stabbing widow's peak and leathery tan broken by whitened scars on either cheek. He looked . . . familiar. She had seen his face somewhere before. But where?

Her gaze went to the girl; she recognized the type instantly. A bargirl like herself, yet harder, with little smarts, a type with little or no chance of being anything more than she was and a huge chance at being less.

It struck her where she had seen the man before, at least his face. His Wanted poster hung in the marshal's office. The fellow was an outlaw named John Barlow.

She stiffened, heart beginning to thud, a gasp escaping her lips. She quickly regained her composure, jamming her hands to her cinched waist.

'We're closed.' She fought to keep her voice steady.

'Are you, now?' Barlow walked towards her, bargirl in tow. His gaze searched the bar-room, finally coming to rest on her. 'Nice place. Sorry I didn't come earlier, but I was . . . detained.'

'Like the lady said, we're closed,' Ben said from behind the bar. 'You'll have to come back tomorrow.'

A sudden tenseness tightened the air and Sam knew Ben had recognized Barlow as well.

Barlow let a smug expression turn his lips. 'Didn't come here to give you no business. I'm lookin' for someone. Maybe you know where I could find her.'

'Her?' Ben cocked an eyebrow.

'A filly named Samantha Dale.'

Samantha chopped a gasp short and Ben's eyes cut to her and as quickly away. Barlow turned to her.

'Well, reckon I found her, haven't I?'

'She's not here. Left hours ago,' Ben said, the lie plain in his voice.

Barlow's gaze snapped to Ben. 'You know who I am, don't you?'

The 'keep remained silent, but the flitter of fear in his eyes answered the question.

Barlow smiled. 'Good, I like it that way. Now you can die knowin' you got yourself killed by a famous outlaw.' Barlow drew his Starr with lightning speed and triggered a shot. A blotch of crimson exploded on the 'keep's shirt. Ben jolted backwards, slamming into a hutch filled with bottles. He went down, bottles crashing around him.

Samantha screamed, hands going to her mouth. The 'keep spasmed, lay still.

'You bastard!' Samantha shrieked, balling her fists and charging Barlow. She swung at his face, but he brought up the Starr's butt in a vicious arc, catching her full across the jaw. Her eyes rolled upward and she collapsed.

Through gauzy blackness, she heard Barlow laugh as he bent over her. 'Looks like we got ourselves a traveling companion, Delaney.'

Delaney's eyes narrowed, jealousy sparking. 'Don't y'all go thinkin' 'bout gettin' too cosy with her, Johnny. Ah know how you git.'

Barlow laughed harder and threw Sam over his shoulder.

* * *

The town had changed somehow. Duel sensed that immediately as he and Elmo trotted into Burton's Bend. Something had changed and not for the better. Although the hour was early, fewer folks lined the boardwalks. Burton's Bend normally burst to life with false dawn. Of the folks out and about, he spotted strained looks and stiffness in their strides. That gave him pause and a knotting dread in his belly. He drew up, signaling Elmo to stop.

'What's wrong?' Elmo asked.

'Dunno.' Duel shook his head. 'Got a bad feeling all of a sudden.'

'I don't see nothin'.'

'Ever been here before?'

'No.'

'Then you probably wouldn't. But I can see it. I can *feel* it.' He slowly straightened in the saddle. 'Barlow . . . '. The name slipped past his lips as his gaze fell upon the partially constructed gallows a piece down the street. He nudged his horse forward, Elmo following suit.

In front of the marshal's office he drew up, dismounting and coming up behind Elmo, who was doing the same. Duel urged Elmo ahead and they entered the office. It was empty. The cells were unoccupied.

A chill shivered down Duel's spine. He saw a dark stain on the floor near the desk. Dread froze him a moment, then he drew a deep breath and glanced at Elmo, who had a worried expression on his face.

'What's wrong?' the smaller man asked.

'That stain . . . blood.'

'Blood?'

'I left someone here with the marshal . . . don't see neither.'

'So?'

'This man was a vicious killer. He was s'posed to be hanged yesterday dawn. Gallows ain't been finished so I reckon he wasn't.'

'I still don't understand.'

Duel eyed Elmo. 'Get in the cell.'

'What?'

'I said get in the cell.' The look in Duel's eyes put Elmo into motion. He stepped into the cell and Duel grabbed the key ring on the desk, closing the door and locking it.

'Where are you going?' Concern laced Elmo's voice.

'Don't worry, I'll be back for you. The man who had this cell before, I have a feeling he escaped and that ain't the news I wanted to hear.'

An understatement, Duel thought, stepping out on to the boardwalk. John Barlow was missing and so was Ben Morrison. Duel knew in his gut that bloodstain belonged to his friend.

Another death on your hands . . .

He felt dread close in on him. More death. He had half-convinced himself it was over, but it was not, not if John Barlow remained alive.

He walked along the boardwalk, gaze scanning the people. He noticed a deputy standing near the doc's office and approached him.

'Duel . . . ' the deputy said, recognizing him.

'Where's Ben Morrison?' Duel asked, grimness in his tone.

The deputy looked down, up. 'He's . . . in the doc's. He ain't so good, Duel. Barlow shot him bad . . . '.

'Barlow?' Duel tensed for the answer.

'Gone. Looks like that woman of his got him out.'

Duel felt his stomach sink. His eyes closed, opened, and he pushed past the deputy. Entering the doc's office, he walked through a small reception room. He found the doc leaning over a bed. In the bed lay Ben Morrison. The doc looked up at the sound of Duel's footsteps.

'You . . . ' said the doc, recognizing Duel from when he'd stopped to get his head gash cleaned up. 'You're the one who brought Barlow in, aren't you?'

Duel wasn't sure whether he heard a note of accusation attached to the question, or if he was feeling his own guilt.

'How is he?' Duel nodded to Morrison.

'Not good. Gutshot pretty bad. Lost enough blood.'

Duel swallowed. 'Will he live?'

The doc shrugged. 'Bullet managed to miss any of his vitals by some miracle, but with the blood loss . . . I can't tell for sure. Won't be too much longer 'fore I know. He'll either die or come out of it at once. If he dies we'll lose a hell of a man, you know.'

'I know better'n anyone. And I'll get the man responsible.'

'You got him once. Didn't do much good.'

The remark stung and he felt his innards tighten. 'Why wasn't Barlow hanged?'

'Didn't finished the gallows in time, but he would have been come sun-down. 'Sides, the damn town wanted to make a show of it. Disgusting if you ask me. Look what it got them.'

'I should have killed him . . . ' Duel mumbled.

'What's that?'

Duel shook his head. 'He awake at all?'

'In and out. You're welcome to try talkin' to him, but not for long. He needs rest.'

Duel nodded, stepping closer to the bed while the doc went to a shelf, pulling down a bottle of laudanum.

'Ben . . . ' Duel whispered.

Morrison's eyelids fluttered open. Duel could see the pain in his friend's eyes, and the gladness at seeing him.

'Duel, you ol' skunk.' Morrison's voice came out low and strained. 'Reckon I let you down . . . '

'You didn't let no one down, Ben. It was me who let you down. I should have killed Barlow. Men like him don't deserve capture.'

'You did . . . what was right.'

'I've spent my whole life trying to do

what was right, Ben. It's only got me death. Now I gotta clean it up.'

'You . . . ' Ben's eyes fluttered closed, opened. 'So dark, Duel, so tired . . . '

'Sleep, Ben. Rest up and you'll be back on the job 'fore you know it.' Duel took his friend's hand, squeezing.

'Duel . . . ' Morrison struggled for words. 'He knows 'bout . . . Sam . . . '

'What?' Duel's eyes widened and his stomach dropped.

'Said, said he was gonna get even with you through her. Don't let him . . . mess up my invitation . . . ' Morrison's eyes closed again and his breathing turned thready. The doc shoved in front of Duel, checking the wounded man.

'You have to go,' he told Duel.

'Is he . . . ?' The words trailed off.

'He's alive, but he needs time, now. If he wakes up he'll probably make it. If not . . . '.

Duel nodded, backing out of the room.

Reaching the street, he paused and

took a deep breath. It wasn't over the way he thought. He should have known better. He should have stayed to see Barlow hang, but he had been so damned eager to get on with his life and get back to Sam. A foolish mistake, one so close to his goal. He knew now why Barlow had told the girl to ask about him, what his plan had been. The outlaw planned to seek revenge by using the one thing Duel cared about: Samantha Dale. Duel had no other attachments. Capturing him had interrupted Barlow's scheme only briefly.

Duel should have paid more attention to the girl.

For the second time Barlow had used her for escape and for the second time Duel had fallen for it. He had reckoned her gone when a search failed to turn her up.

The next time you make a mistake like that you'll be dead.

Maybe he already was. If Barlow got to Samantha, hurt her . . . well, Duel could see no life for himself without her.

He made his way back to the marshal's office. Elmo looked up as he came in.

Duel grabbed the key ring and opened the cell door.

'You're comin' with me.' He motioned Elmo out.

'Where're we going?' Elmo carried a perpetually worried expression, now.

'I brought in an outlaw by the name of John Barlow — '

'Barlow! God almighty, you're better'n I thought.'

'You heard of him?'

'Anyone who hasn't?'

'He escaped. He's headed towards a town south of here. He intends to go after someone . . . I have to stop him. You'll ride with me and keep up or I'll shoot you 'fore the mayor gets the chance.'

Elmo clamped his mouth shut and followed Duel out to the horses. Duel stepped into the saddle and reined around, Elmo following suit.

John Barlow had a decent head start on him and Duel reckoned he could reach Whitehead Pass by sundown if he pushed it. Elmo might slow him up, but he knew Barlow would have hit town during the night and what was to happen already had. Duel prayed the outlaw had not harmed her. He reckoned odds were the hardcase would keep her alive and bait Duel into something. At least that's what he'd tell himself over and over until they reached Whitehead Pass.

6

The sun had slipped deep into the west by the time Duel and Elmo stopped by a stream to water and rest the horses. Duel climbed from the saddle, the swelling dread inside him growing stronger the closer they drew to Whitehead Pass. Barlow had beaten him there, no question about that, but what had the outlaw done after his arrival? Sam would be his first order of business. While Duel felt sure the hardcase would keep her alive for some vengeful purpose, he found it hard to predict what the man might do to her in the meantime. Duel felt only a twinge of relief the other bargirl was with them. That might prevent some of the things Barlow had been known to do to women from happening to Sam.

How long would Barlow keep Sam alive? It stood to reason the outlaw had more in mind than merely luring Duel somewhere to kill him. Barlow would want to savor his revenge. To do that he would use what was dearest to Duel: Sam.

He's waiting to kill her until you can watch her die.

The thought made him shudder, but he bet it was on the mark.

He knelt beside the stream, splashing cool water into his face. Elmo scooched nearby, doing the same. The ride had been long and hard but the fake preacher had kept up, uncharacteristically quiet.

'You're worried about her,' Elmo said, facing Duel, face dripping.

'More than worried, Elmo. It's eatin' a hole in my gut.'

'I'm told that kind of worry ain't good for a man in your . . . well, profession.'

'No, it ain't. It means I don't belong doin' what I'm doin' no more. Means I got things tyin' me down and when you got that, the enemy has the advantage.'

'Reckon it's more than that.'

'Meanin'?' Duel eyed the smaller man.

Elmo shrugged. 'You an' me, we're a lot alike, you know, least in some ways.'

'How you figure?'

'Just that we're always searchin' for something we couldn't see. You ridin' from place to place, never settling, but maybe deep down wanting to more than anything. And me, going from woman to woman . . . I always wanted to find one, you know.'

'A woman?'

Elmo frowned. 'A woman.'

'Seems like you had more than your share.'

'Maybe so. But none were what I wanted. I mean, I wanted to find me someone I could stay with and never need to go searchin' again.'

'You ain't likely to find that with saloon gals.'

'Didn't you?' Elmo met his gaze and Duel found himself without a response. True, he had found it with a saloon girl and maybe he was plumb wrong to go judgin' Elmo when he didn't really know the man. In fact, he discovered himself liking the smaller man more and more. Although Elmo tended to be an annoyance, as well as a philanderer, Duel found the company strangely welcome. He'd spent countless nights on the trail alone and, yes, searching the way Elmo said. He'd been too pig-headed to realize what he searched for lay with a woman named Samantha Dale, and now all that was at risk.

'Yes, I surely did. But maybe it's too late for me, Elmo. You still got a chance. Think on it before you find yourself at the wrong end of a rope.'

'That's just where the mayor'll have me if he gets his way.'

Duel gave a chuckle. 'We'll see . . . '

Elmo looked at him with a puzzled expression. Duel stood, taking a deep breath. He went to his horse, mounting and grabbing the reins tightly. Elmo wandered to his horse and stepped into the saddle.

'She must be a hell of a woman to make a difference to a man like you.' The man with the high voice gave Duel a serious look.

Duel smiled, seeing her face in his mind. 'That she is . . . but maybe I ain't such a hell of a man.'

He gigged his horse into a canter and Elmo followed suit. They rode for the better part of an hour. The sun sank lower in the sky and clawing shadows crept across the land. With the first sight of Whitehead Pass, Duel felt the knot in his belly tighten, one of vague fear mixed with remorse and nostalgia. Whitehead Pass. It had been better'n a year since he left but still it brought a bitter-sweet melancholy to his soul. It was a cowtown, not so far from the Pecos, the same as a hundred other such towns scattered across the valley. While men like John Chisum carved out their huge cattle empires, towns like Whitehead Pass sprang up like toad-stools, rife with the pleasures of sin, eager to bleed tired cowhands of their thirty-a-month pay. Not that the cowhands complained. They got their money's worth: whiskey, women and wagers. Duel had spent plenty of time in towns like this himself, maybe searching for just the thing Elmo had mentioned. Or at least trying to fill the emptiness he had felt eating a hole in his being.

Who could say he had not found that? He had found Sam. But now . . . well, would it make a lick of difference? He hoped to God it would.

He drew up, eyeing the town, the streets strangely subdued compared to the last time he'd been through. Barlow had been here. Duel felt as sure of that as he ever felt of anything. Only towns Barlow passed through carried that stain of somberness, that sense of being brushed by evil.

He turned to Elmo, leaning his forearms on the horn. 'You said you believed in what you were sayin' . . . '

Elmo pulled a tattered Bible from his pocket, a tiny thing with pages sticking out. 'You mean this?'

Duel nodded.

'Yeah, I do. I swear to you that's God honest truth. Maybe it don't make up for the things I done and maybe it never will, but I reckon it's my belief.'

'Maybe you don't have to make up for it, Elmo; maybe you just gotta stop.'

'I hope you're right, Duel Winston. 'cause right now I'm startin' to see things in a different light. Seein' the way you been thinkin' about her, well, I want the same thing and I reckon I just might have been lookin' in the wrong places.'

Duel gave a pinched smile. 'Like I said, I ain't never been a godly man, Elmo, but right now I'd appreciate it if you said a little prayer for her. She don't deserve what a man like Barlow can do.'

Elmo nodded. 'I'll throw in one for you while I'm at it.'

'Obliged . . . ' Duel dug his heels into the bay's sides and the animal charged forward. Elmo pocketed the Bible and set his sorrel into motion.

Duel focused on the town, not giving the worry of whether Barlow was waiting for him a whole lot of consideration. He slowed as he entered the side main street, surveying the saloons and gambling houses, stores and offices. Folks were out and about, but subdued. Usually by this time of day there was a flurry of activity.

'You're right in what you're thinkin',' said Elmo.

'What's that?'

'Barlow's been here, all right. You can tell by the way these folks look, like they was scared of him comin' back. It's like . . . ' Elmo cut his words off.

'Like someone died,' Duel finished.

Elmo nodded. 'Maybe you better say an extra prayer.'

Duel said one himself. For Samantha. For the hell of it, he asked the Devil to pull John Barlow's marker early.

He stopped in front of a saloon, the knot in his belly making him feel as if he'd been kicked by a mule. The place was closed and that made his legs go weak. Dismounting, he tethered his bay to the rail. Elmo stepped down and came up beside him.

'This where she worked?'

Duel nodded almost imperceptibly. 'It's closed.' He felt himself strangely reluctant to discover what had happened, a feeling he wasn't at all used to. It made him uncomfortable. It reinforced what he had known all along: he would never get used to death, only more repulsed by it, at least the violent death men like John Barlow — and himself — brought. He'd spent years trying to banish the memory of his parents' deaths by delivering more death, couched in the trappings of justice. It all amounted to the same thing and those souls haunted him now. Would hers haunt him as well?

'Duel Winston!'

The voice startled him, snapping the spell. He whirled, hand slapping for the Peacemaker in a blur of motion. The gun cleared leather, leveling on a target he knew stood directly behind him.

A man wearing a badge gasped, stiffening in fear, and Duel's lips parted slightly. 'Marshal . . . .'

'A mite jumpy on that, ain'tcha?' the marshal said, recovering his composure.

Duel looked at the gun in his hand, holstered it. 'Sorry, Fred. Reckon I am a mite jumpy at that. But I got call to be.'

'I guess you do.' The marshal stepped closer, proffering his hand. 'It's been a long time, Duel. More than a year, if I recollect right. Thought you'd get back this way eventually. Sam figured sooner, I figured later. I'm glad she was right.'

Duel wasted no time with small talk. 'I was on my way back, anyhow, but now I got a different reason.'

The marshal nodded. 'I figured as much. Can tell by the way you drew that piece.'

'John Barlow.' The name hung in the

air after Duel spoke it. The marshal shuddered. Duel's heart thudded mildly, nerves raw.

'He was here all right.' The marshal's face went tight and his eyes lowered, came up.

'Is she . . . ?' Duel let the words trail off, emotion choking his throat.

'She's gone, Duel. He took her. Him and some bargirl came in and killed the barkeep last night. Shot some drunk cowhand on the way out just for the hell of it. I ain't never seen the likes of a man that snake-blooded.'

Duel seemed to deflate, half-horrified at the news, half-relieved because the marshal had confirmed Barlow hadn't killed Sam right away. 'Likely you won't ever again, Fred. Anybody see which way they went?'

'Couple fellas saw them ride west. He picked up an extra horse at the livery free of expense, so to speak, and put Sam on it. Looked like he had hit her from the tellin' of it, but she was alive, stirrin' as they rode out. I learned of it this mornin' when I got back from Matadero.'

'West . . . ' Duel muttered. He had a notion —

'Left you a message, Duel. Least now I realize it was for you. At the time I wondered.'

'What is it?'

The marshal eyed Duel in the deepening shadows of dusk. He moved past the two men and opened the saloon door, going inside. He fired a lantern and set it on the bar counter. 'There . . . ' The marshal pointed, and Duel's gaze lifted to the huge gilt-edged mirror behind the bar. Across its front was a word smeared in dried blood: Tumbleweed.

Duel nodded, coldness swarming through him. His notion had been confirmed: Barlow had left word of his whereabouts, knowing only one man would be foolish enough to follow him into hell.

'That's the barkeep's blood the bastard wrote it in.' A sickened look crossed the marshal's face. 'You reckon you know what it means?'

'He's waiting for me in Tumbleweed, with Sam . . . '

'Tumbleweed's a ghost town,' Elmo put in, brow scrunching. 'Barlow made it one.'

'Reckon Barlow wants privacy when he kills me . . . ' hint of sarcasm laced Duel's voice. 'Wants me where he can do what he pleases with nothing interfering.'

'You ain't goin' there . . . ' the marshal said in a worried voice.

'He has to,' Elmo answered, voice somber. 'It's the end of the trail.'

The marshal led the way back to his office. Duel had no desire to stay in the barroom any longer than necessary. The sense of death, of grimness, hung too heavy in the air.

In the marshal's office, the lawman lit a lantern and Duel looked at Elmo, then the marshal. 'I want you to do me a favor, Fred.'

'Name it, Duel. Ain't likely I'll be

seein' you again and it's the least I can do.'

'You don't give Mr Winston much credit.' There was no sense of surety in Elmo's voice either.

'Not that. I know Duel's the best there is at what he does. But John Barlow's the best at his trade, too, and he plays by a whole lot meaner set of rules. He's got the advantage. He's got a town he knows and a woman Duel loves. That makes the odds in his favor if they weren't already.'

'He's right,' Duel said. 'I know what I'm up against, but if I'm gonna die, John Barlow's gonna take the trip to hell with me.'

'Name your favor, Duel,' the marshal said.

'Put Elmo in a cell.'

'What?' Elmo blurted. 'At least let me go with you.'

Duel almost laughed at the man's utter seriousness. His respect for the smaller man jumped another notch. He had sand, more than most. But that fact made him feel all the more right about his decision.

'Why would you want to do that, Elmo?'

'Mayor's gonna kill me anyhow.' Elmo's voice came resigned, somber. 'If I got to die I'd rather do it with a chance at redemption and helpin' you would give me that chance.'

Duel shook his head. 'No, I gotta do this alone. Barlow sees you ride in with me, he'll kill you instantly.' Duel motioned to the marshal and the lawman guided Elmo into a cell and locked the door.

Duel pulled out a roll of bills and handed a few to the marshal. 'See to it Millie gives this fella the best she's got in grub. I ain't back in a week, he's free to go.'

The lawman nodded, taking the money. 'Will do.'

Duel went to the door.

'Good luck,' the marshal said, as Duel looked back to Elmo and tipped his hat.

'I'll need it . . . '.

7

The ride to Tumbleweed would take most of the night. Duel knew he couldn't ride his mount that hard after making the journey from Burton's Bend to Whitehead Pass so he went to the livery and boarded his bay. Selecting a sturdy chestnut, he paid the attendant, then took the time to stop at an eatery and force down a meal of beefsteak and fried potatoes, washed down with strong coffee. He wasn't particularly hungry despite the long day on the trail, belly twisted in knots, but he would need his strength for what lay ahead. John Barlow would wait the extra half-hour it took him to eat. While the outlaw was unpredictable in many ways, Duel knew the delay wouldn't make a difference. He would make no moves until Duel walked into his trap.

Duel finished his meal and hit the

saddle. He set his chestnut at a steady gait, feeling the big animal's muscles ripple beneath him.

He rode for the better part of three hours before stopping near a stream and making camp. He desperately needed a few hours' sleep before facing Barlow. Exhaustion gripped him and he felt every bump and bounce with the force of a blow. His muscles ached and his tailbone bitched and if he pushed himself to make the trek without rest he would be in little shape to face the hardcase. He was at enough of a disadvantage as it was. Barlow was a powerful man, no doubt rested and ready and holding an ace: Sam. Duel knew a man at any less than his full game usually met with doom and against Barlow that was doubled.

He dismounted, tethering the horse to a tree and went to the stream. Bending, he splashed water into his face and wiped off with his bandanna. He knelt for long minutes, staring at his reflection in the glossy-dark water sprinkled with captured starlight. Standing, he peered at the horizon. The dark shapes of brush and scrub trees loomed over swaying shadows. He swore he glimpsed Barlow's face in every swell of blackness, heard the outlaw's mocking laughter echo across the breeze. It was truly a land of ghosts, all waiting to snatch him up if he stumbled, made a mistake.

Kill or be killed . . .

A code he had lived by and would a last time. John Barlow would die, even if it meant his own death. He realized now nothing could bring his parents' deaths to peace in his mind, not the death of one outlaw, not the deaths of a hundred. Not John Barlow's. The chance of losing Sam made him recognize he had chased an empty promise. Some things could never be laid to peace, and those things, bitter as hell as they were, had to be accepted and lived with. If not they simply rotted away your own chance at living, and he'd let them eat away too much of his. The realization may have come too late, but he would not let the chance — or her — go without a hell of a fight. A man the likes of Duel Winston might never be granted peace, but he was damned if he'd let John Barlow stand in the way of acceptance, and he was damned if he'd let the hardcase soak his conscience with Sam's blood.

He reckoned he could live with anything but that.

Duel unrolled his bedding and settled in after building a fire. Drifting in and out of a disturbed sleep, he found his dreams crowded with nightmarish images of the outlaw and Sam and death. Each killing from his past played itself out with bitter grimness in his mind and each departed soul revisited him. Within each ghost he saw the ghoulish form of John Barlow. He awoke with a start, sweat streaming down his face, heart thundering, shadows reaching. He forced himself to breathe evenly, sitting with his face in his hands for long moments.

Finally standing, he gulped the rest of the coffee he'd made and broke camp. He hadn't gotten the rest he wanted but he reckoned broken sleep was better than none.

In the saddle once more, he stared out across the terrain, watching the shadows shift with ribbons of moonlight. The darkness, the ghosts called to him, entreating and darkly wanton. Miles distant lay Tumbleweed, a town Barlow had destroyed and now haunted. A ghost town, in which dwelled a man as inhuman as any Duel had met.

'I'm coming, you sonofabitch . . . ' His whisper floated across the wind.

* * *

The sunrise painted the heavens with a blaze of orange and yellow and glossed Whitehead Pass with streamers of light. Early risers began to move about, unconsciously avoiding the saloon. Dusty light shafted through its windows, illuminating the gruesome blood letters on the mirror. That aside, life went on close to normal in Whitehead Pass and eventually the stain of dread left by John Barlow would be scrubbed nearly clean.

Except for Elmo.

In the marshal's office sunlight swelled into the cell and Elmo drew a deep breath. Sleep had proved elusive much of the night. His handsome face had grown drawn, eyes rimmed with black circles. He swung his feet off the cot and eyed the marshal, who slept in a chair behind the desk, hat pulled over his face. The marshal stirred, grumbled, with the lightening of the room, pushed his hat to the top of his head.

'You're awake bright and early,' the lawman said, rubbing sleep from his eyes.

'So are you.'

'Reckon I been thinkin' mostly 'bout what Duel's likely to run into when he gets to Tumbleweed.'

'Reckon I have, too.'

The marshal stood, stretching and yawning. 'I'm headin' over to the eatery. I'll send Millie over in a few minutes with your breakfast. She makes the best fried taters you ever et. You're in for a treat.' The lawman walked out, leaving Elmo alone with his thoughts.

Thinking: that's something he had done much of in the last two days. He'd reached some conclusions, thanks to Duel Winston, a man he'd grown to respect and admire not a little since their 'association'. He could wait the week, see whether Duel returned, and be a free man. But he would just be hunted by some other tracker if Duel didn't come back. The mayor wouldn't rest until Elmo was at the end of a noose or shot dead. That left him little choice, indeed.

The door opened and a middle-aged woman with blonde-brown hair stepped through, carrying a tray stacked with food. Elmo looked her over, noting she was attractive in a matronly sort of way. A smile oiled his lips. She returned the smile and came closer to the cell, sliding the tray through the slot at the bottom.

'Mornin', ma'am,' Elmo said, tipping an imaginary hat.

'Marshal said you could use some breakfast.'

'I surely could at that, my fine lady. Ah, tell me if you'd be so kind, what day is it?'

'Why, sir, it's the Lord's Day, Sunday. I have to be gettin' myself over to the church right soon.'

Elmo preened his hair and reached into a pocket, bringing out the stiff white collar and clamping it about his throat. 'Why, no need, ma'am, no need . . . ' His smile widened and Millie smiled back . . .

* * *

Tumbleweed grinned like a skull on the horizon. Its shambly affair of buildings stretched out like weathered bones. A dead town, picked clean; even the buzzards had moved on. Duel Winston felt his blood chill at the sight, a grim reflection of the man he faced, the results he could bring. He swallowed, throat dry, tensing in the saddle. He had reached it, stood face to face with his fate. Barlow awaited him in that corrupted town; more than like, one or both men would not leave it alive.

He prayed Sam would.

The brassy sun beat down on him, drawing sweat; it ran into his eyes, stinging, slithered down his sides and belly. In his vision the town blurred, shimmered under waves of heat rippling off the desert. The bones and skull distorted, as if laughing, reaching. A sidewinder slithered off to the left, angling into a patch of scrubby sage that jutted from the parched earth. He slowed, dread swelling. He felt as close to fear as he ever had.

The town seemed to swallow him as he rode into the main street. Arid breeze kicked up spectres of dust, moaned through deserted buildings. Tumbleweeds cartwheeled across the street with scratchy sounds, leaving claw-like trails in the dirt. A haunting feeling took him, like the strange stillness that follows death. Emptiness. A town with no soul. Like the man who had fashioned it.

Duel tightened his grip on the reins. Barlow was here, but where? The town appeared deserted. The buildings, some in shambles, boards hanging loose, wooden awnings ready for collapse, mocked him in mute testimony. Windows were busted out, some boarded over. Dust lay thick on the boardwalks. Somewhere he caught the dice-shake sound of a rattler.

He drew up, scanning every direction for a clue to Barlow's whereabouts. Nothing. No glint of sunlight from gunmetal, no sign of tracks; all had been scrubbed clean by shifting sand and scorching wind. Fury swelled within him, overriding his caution.

'Barlow!' he shouted, voice echoing like goblins laughing from the dilapidated buildings. 'Barlow, you sonofabitch, where are you?'

The breeze answered, raspy. The sun pounded his body and sweat crawled over his skin, irritating him. A tumbleweed scritched across the boardwalk. His fury increased.

'Barlow, you coward! I came like you wanted. Let her go! I'll give you anything you want.'

'I want your soul, Duel Winston!' a voice echoed back, and Duel stiffened. The voice seemed to reverberate from everywhere at once and Duel couldn't pin down a direction.

'Let Sam go!' Duel answered.

A laugh swelled back, more directional, to the right. Duel's gaze rose; he felt sure Barlow was poised slightly ahead of him. He studied each building corner and roof top, but saw nothing.

'I can't do that, bounty man. I know you got a thing for the gal. Made it my business to know everything about you.

You shoulda called it quits before getting around to me. You should have thought it over then, Winston. Now, it's too late! I'm gonna kill you, but not before I make you suffer.'

'If you harm her . . . '

'You ain't in the position to go makin' no threats, bounty man. Fact is, I ain't gonna have a whole hell of a lot of use for the lady right soon. Kill her for sure then, but you ain't gonna know when. Reckon I'll be so kind as to let you watch her die so you can see what a mistake you made the day you signed on to track me down. Reckon your death will serve notice to any bounty man who gets the fool-ass notion to do the same.'

A shot rang out. It took Duel utterly by surprise and he had no chance to avoid it. A bullet ploughed into his shoulder, kicking him back off the horse. He slammed into the ground, air bucked from his lungs, a cloud of dust billowing.

His horse reared in panic, and

bolted. The echo of retreating hoofbeats pounded in his ears.

Half-stunned, Duel struggled to push himself up. Pain seared his shoulder. Blood ran freely from the wound, soaking the front of his shirt. He caught the glint of gunmetal atop a roof ahead of him and a second shot sounded, gouging dirt near his feet.

Barlow missed on purpose that time. If he had wanted to kill Duel immediately, Duel would have had no chance.

Gaining unsteady legs, Duel gripped his shoulder and stumbled sideways to the boardwalk.

'Go on, bounty man! Run and hide! I ain't gonna do ya now. I'm gonna wait, have me some fun. When I come for you it ain't gonna be so quick.'

Duel considered drawing his Peacemaker, firing at the place he'd seen the glint of light. It would be a nearly impossible hit. Barlow had a rifle and the sun angle in his favor. Duel could barely see through the glare and sweat trickling into his eyes.

A third shot made up his mind. The bullet ricocheted from the ground close to his feet and he scooted sideways, clutching his shoulder. He headed left, boots clomping over the dusty boards. Another shot tore splinters inches in front of him. He reversed direction, staggering as weakness crept over him.

Three buildings loomed in front of him, two boarded over, the third a saloon, windows missing. He went for it, shots following his steps, chewing up wood, lodging in walls. Laughter shuddered through the street, taunting.

He fell against the saloon door, forcing it open, kicking it shut behind him. Barlow put a few slugs into it. Then the rifle fire and laughter stopped.

An eerie silence filled the barroom. Duel heard the thudding of his own heart, the throbbing of his pulse in his ears, but nothing else. He staggered to the bar, leaning heavily against the counter, breathing in staggered gasps.

Barlow would leave him be for a spell; he was sure of that. The outlaw wanted him to suffer and this was just the beginning. Duel didn't know when the next move would come. For the time being it didn't matter. He had to get the bullet out of his arm or he'd get no chance at a counter attack.

He made his way around the counter, searching through shattered bottles behind the bar until he managed to find a whiskey bottle that hadn't been broken. He slumped down, his back pressed against the counter, and drew a deep breath. His senses tumbled. He was close to blacking out, so he had to act fast.

He twisted the cap from the bottle with his teeth, spitting it out and swallowing a deep gulp of redeye. The liquor burned his throat and he gasped, coughed, but felt his senses steady.

He fumbled with the bandanna at his neck, soaking it with whiskey, then pulling out his bowie knife and dousing the blade. Gritting his teeth, he tore away part of his shirt at the shoulder, exposing the wound.

Blood flow had slowed and the wound appeared clean. Clutching a breath, he pressed the top of the blade into his flesh. A groan escaped his clenched teeth and sweat streamed down his face. A sliver of white-hot pain shot down to his hand and it was all he could do to hold the knife steady. Pressing the tip into the soft flesh farther, he located the slug with a minimum of probing. The bullet wasn't deep and he manoeuvered the blade tip under it, lifted. He pressed his eyelids closed as spikes of pain radiated down his arm and through his chest. The bullet clattered on the floor and Duel gasped, jerking breaths. He fumbled for the whiskey-drenched cloth and pressed it to the wound.

Agony bit deep into his chest and arm. Blood poured freely from beneath the bandanna. Weakness invaded his body. If he didn't do something about the blood flow he might well bleed to death before Barlow got a second chance at him.

He gained unsteady legs and, bringing the knife and whiskey bottle, staggered to the back of the room. Locating the rear exit, he went out into an alley littered with old crates and barrels. He gathered an armload of wood scraps from shattered crates, dousing them with whiskey. Digging a lucifer from his pocket, he set the pile aflame.

Dropping down beside the fire, he held the knife blade in the flames until it grew red hot. Leaning back against the building, not giving himself a chance to think about it, he pulled the blade from the fire and pressed the flat of it to the bleeding wound.

A scream tore from his lips. The stench of searing flesh assailed his nostrils and deep welts of agony stabbed his shoulder.

The flow of blood slowed to a trickle and he dropped the knife. Pain shocked Duel into a strange sense of alertness.

Everything around him took on jagged, unreal outlines. He suddenly glimpsed figures, men and women flittering past the alley, a barkeep heaving a crate atop another, even John Barlow peering into the alley, grinning. The figures dissolved in diamond sparkles of sunlight, merely images concocted by a fevered mind. The surroundings grew fuzzy, darkening. With numbing fingers, he tied the bandanna around the wound as best he could.

Breathing in raspy gasps, he let his head fall against his chest. 'Sam . . . ' he whispered, not sure if he had spoken at all, as his senses went black.

* * *

John Barlow stood in front of Duel, face replaced by a gleaming skull. Dark holes surrounded by cracked bone punctuated either cheek. The death's head mouth gaped, slack and shuddering with laughter. Vicious glints of light twinkled from hollow black sockets.

Duel was still in the alley, back against the wall. He struggled to stand, but couldn't. The surroundings were murky, darkened. Dull light came from some undisclosed source.

'You're too late, bounty man,' the skull said, voice hollow, chilling. As Barlow stepped forward, diffused light fell over the limp form draped over his arms. Samantha! Her throat slashed, blood soaking her bodice, emerald eyes opened wide, glazed, dull as jade, damning.

'You let me die, Duel,' she said, gaping mouth unmoving. Duel felt swelling terror and guilt. 'You let me die because you wouldn't take me away with you. I begged you, Duel. I begged you. It's your fault . . . '

'My . . . fault . . . ' Duel mumbled, mouth cottony, reaching out for her. Barlow snatched her away.

'None of this would have happened if you'd let me be and gone back to her, bounty man!' Barlow waved his Starr, Sam's body suddenly gone from his arms. Duel's gaze met the outlaw's black sockets. Within flashed images of death and carnage and Duel's past. He witnessed his parents' deaths, felt the terror and horror he'd felt then. Breath clutched in his throat. 'You had your chance, bounty man. Now it's over.'

Barlow lifted the Starr. His finger jerked the trigger — once, twice, three times!

The slugs punched into Duel's chest but he felt no pain. He looked down, shock welding on to his face, to see bloodless holes.

'You're dead, bounty man. Godammit, don't you know that? You're dead and you still can't save her!' Barlow suddenly had Samantha's body in his arms again. He threw her form to the ground; it landed in a lifeless heap at Duel's feet. A scream tore from his throat —

'*Nooo!*'

Duel snapped awake, clamping the scream short. Darkness hovered all around him, pounding with the thundering of his heartbeat. His muscles felt cramped and the small of his back throbbed. Deep pain burned his shoulder.

He made out the vague outlines of crates and barrels and realized he'd blacked out in the alley. Barlow had been merely a nightmare, delirium. His shirt was soaked with sweat and his hair was damp. He reckoned fever had taken him, but had broken.

The fire had burned to ashes and occasional snapping embers. The cool night air gave him a chill but he was thankful for it.

He attempted to move, finding his limbs stiff and unforgiving of the position he'd passed out in. A spike of pain stabbed his shoulder. His fingers went to the wound. The blood had dried and caked; the wound no longer bled.

He forced himself to his feet, jamming his back against the wall and heaving with his legs. A chore, but he managed it, at last leaning heavily against the wall and drawing long breaths. His strength seemed to be returning, but he wasn't up to much movement.

A scuffing sound took his attention. Something moved nearby in the darkness. He felt it more than saw it. A shoe scraped in the dust; trousers swished.

Barlow?

His hand moved to the butt of his Peacemaker; he eased the weapon from its holster and whirled. A burst of dizziness assailed him and darkness spun. He felt his legs go weak, threatening to send him to his knees. Through sheer will he held his ground, thumbing the hammer back.

'Who's there?' he demanded in a hoarse whisper.

A figure came from the darkness. 'Duel?' a high voice whispered.

'Elmo . . . ' Duel felt relief flood him.

'Don't shoot.'

Duel couldn't have shot had he wanted to. The Peacemaker dropped from his fingers and Duel fell against the wall. Elmo scooted over, retrieving the gun and bowie knife beside it, shoving them into Duel's holster and sheath. He jammed an arm under Duel's arms and guided him into the saloon.

Helping Duel to the bar, he lowered him behind the counter, then moved off. Locating a lantern, he set it aglow with a low flame. He squatted in front of Duel after setting the lantern on the floor and foraging for another intact bottle of whiskey. Opening it, he passed it to Duel, who drank deeply, then handed it back to Elmo. Elmo took a swig and thunked the bottle down.

Sweat beaded on Duel's brow, running freely down his face. 'How the hell d'you get outa that cell?'

Elmo grinned. 'Millie's a right fine-lookin' woman for a gal of her years. Seems she hasn't had much in the way of menfolk in quite a spell.' Elmo slumped against the wall.

Duel smiled, for once thankful for Elmo's way with the ladies. 'Why'd you come here? You could have run.'

'Where would I go? If you got yourself killed I'd be runnin' from the mayor forever. He'd get some other bounty hunter to track me down. Reckon I want to change and I figured you could help me out on that account, maybe talk to the mayor. He'll hang me for sure, Duel. I wasn't lyin' when I told you that.'

'I believe you. We get out of this alive I'll see to it you get a clean slate, no matter what the mayor says. I got some friends higher than him. Done them some turns; reckon they can do the like for me.'

'Thanks, Duel; I mean that.'

'How'd you get in without Barlow spottin' you?'

'I stopped my horse a ways from the town and walked in quietlike. Left the mount in the livery and started lookin' around. It was dark and sneakin's a specialty of mine. I heard you yell out in the alley and figured that was the way to head.'

'Glad you did, Elmo. Reckon I could use the help.'

'How bad is it?' Elmo nudged his head at the wound.

'Seen worse. Hell, had worse. Bleedin's stopped, but it'll hurt like a sonofabitch for a spell. I should be better after a little sleep.'

'Reckon you can sleep while I keep watch.'

'Appreciate it.' Duel beckoned for the whiskey and Elmo passed it to him. The fiery liquor oiled his throat, settled in his gut with warm fire. It was probably the worst rotgut he had ever tasted but at the moment that made no difference to him.

'Where's Barlow?' Elmo asked, voice going somber.

'He's here, somewhere, hiding. Reckon I'll start looking for him tomorrow. He's got Sam but I think she's alive for the moment. He wants me to suffer a spell 'fore he finishes it.'

'Appears he's got a decent start on that.'

'He could've killed me right off. I wasn't usin' my head and he had a clear shot. But he didn't and I figure that gives me a chance to return the favor.'

'You believe that? I mean, you ain't up to full speed now and Barlow's a bad *hombre* even for the best.'

'Ain't got a whole hell of a lot of choice.' Duel eyed the younger man, thankful for his presence, though he had wanted to go this alone.

'Promise me one thing, Elmo . . . '

'What's that?' Elmo took a swig of whiskey.

'I don't care what happens to me, but I want Sam to come out of this alive. I have to finish Barlow and he has to finish me. No way 'round that. If the cards fall right, I want you to get her away from here. Get her away and never look back. See to it she's taken care of.'

'I'll do my best, Duel. I promise you that.'

Duel let a small smile filter on to his lips. It wasn't much of a hope, but it was something. He forced himself not to think about the poor odds of getting Sam out. He had to focus on the positive or give in to Barlow's plan for suffering. He felt weakness wander through him again, and a fuzziness at the edge of his mind. He drew his Peacemaker, handing it to Elmo.

'Reckon I ain't gonna be awake much longer, Elmo. Shoot anything that comes through the door.'

'Don't worry, Barlow comes in here he's a dead man . . . '

8

Duel Winston awoke just before dawn. Gauzy-grey light filtered through the jagged shards of dusty glass dangling from the window frames. It fell across the sawdust- and dirt-carpeted floor in sharp outlines slicing into shadows. Motes twirled in a shaft of dim light and the barroom took on the feel of an undertaker's parlor. The feeling pleased him not in the least. Because that's what this room stood high chance of becoming for him and Elmo — a death room, where the echoes of dying breaths lived on with the murmur of lost hopes and dreams of those who had died here when Barlow made this town his own. Unless Duel found Barlow first.

Duel's gaze shifted to Elmo, who still clutched the Peacemaker and was eyeing the room himself, a frown creasing his lips.

Duel ran his tongue over dry lips; the sour taste of stale whiskey and grit lay heavy in his mouth.

'No one tried to come in,' Elmo said, shifting position and handing the Peacemaker back to Duel.

Duel nodded, holstering the weapon. 'He's out there, waiting, making me wonder what he'll do next. It's part of his plan. He knows while he has Sam it'll wear my nerves raw and that'll give him all the more satisfaction.'

'When you reckon he'll stop playing with you and try for the kill?' Elmo's eyes looked heavy, but filled with worry.

'Eventually. Who knows with a man like Barlow? Thought I had me a line on near to every type of outlaw, but Barlow, he's different. Sneakier than most and meaner. Luckier, too. He lays down a pattern and steps out of it. Fooled me twice and I reckon part of that was me. I can't let it happen again.'

'You plan to sit here till he comes for you or you got a plan?'

'I'm not aimin' to sit around; that'd make it too easy for him. I'm gonna try goin' out there and see what I can find. He knows this town, but he can't be everywhere at once.'

'He's probably watchin' you.'

'Likely. But he's got Sam and another gal with him; that's gonna take his attention, too. Just pray he's busy with that when I do.'

'I'm goin' with you.'

Duel eyed the man, seeing raw courage swell in his eyes. He conceded he'd made a mistake thinking Elmo to be merely a philanderer and easy mark. The man carried a deep courage and loyalty and even a peculiar code of honesty Duel wouldn't have figured on. If they survived this, Duel was determined to see Elmo let free of all charges and give up the bounty.

But surviving was a big question mark. Would Barlow be watching when they tried to leave the saloon? Duel reckoned he would. But what action would the outlaw take? Barlow likely figured himself untouchable in Tumbleweed, a town of his own design. That might make him complacent. If that proved the case, Duel would jump on the advantage.

'That's your choice, Elmo. I ain't gonna hold you back no more. Far as I'm concerned, you're a free man. My advice would be to take yourself as far away from here as you can.'

Elmo's features took on a determined look. 'I made you a promise and I aim to stick to it. To be honest, ain't much out there for me anyways, not with the mayor doggin' me.'

Duel smiled thinly. He pushed himself to his feet, stiff muscles objecting. He'd spent the night in one position, back propped against the bar; it hadn't done him any good. He steadied himself, slowly stretching and getting the circulation back into his limbs. The small of his back ached and the wound set up with a dull throbbing. He took a deep breath, finding he could move his arm somewhat despite the pain in his shoulder. He felt stronger with sleep, but not at full speed. He grabbed the whiskey bottle, Elmo looking up at him.

'Breakfast,' Duel said with a sideways grin, taking a gulp. 'Horse ran off with all my provisions.'

'Got me some on mine.'

'Good. That's the first place we head after we look around. No tellin' how long it'll be 'fore Barlow gets around to us and I wouldn't put it past him to figure on starvin' me till I start seein' things.'

Duel went to the shattered window. Brass sunlight swelled over the horizon, glinting off the dust in the wide main street and from the remains of windows. The surroundings looked utterly deserted except for tumbleweeds and sprites of stirred dust. He spotted no sign of Barlow, nor did he expect to. The hardcase would likely wait till Duel had been softened up to a point where the outlaw had no chance of being out-drawn or outmanoeuvered

Duel moved away from the window, going to the back door and opening it. He scanned the alley. Elmo wandered up behind him.

'Anything?'

Duel slowly shook his head, drawing his Peacemaker. His fingers clamped tight of the grip and when he looked down they were white. He carried none of his usual calmness, none of that steel-nerved determination. Too much was at stake this time and he felt too worn. Win or lose against Barlow, his career as a bounty hunter had come to an end and he knew it.

He edged out into the alley, Elmo following closely.

* * *

The trapdoor in the floor of the bank vault popped open and John Barlow climbed from the ladder into the small chamber. It was a tunnel he, with the help of some temporary gang members — all of whom had met with unfortunate 'accidents' after the completion of the tunnel — had constructed shortly after arriving in Tumbleweed six years ago. Along with others, located at various spots about Tumbleweed, the tunnel was to serve as an escape route and hideout, be part of a network he envisioned would make him invincible to the law — but that was before the law became scared of him. But he had made a miscalculation. Cowards as they were, the ones not dead by his hand, that is, the fine folks had pulled stakes, abandoned Tumbleweed, leaving him with little more than a dust pit. But he supposed the place had turned out to have some use after all. He retreated here sometimes, even kept supplies built up in case of a long stay, though he had reckoned no one would ever have the sand to pursue him.

But there was a fool at every dance. Duel Winston wasn't like the other lawmen and bounty hunters Barlow had encountered. Most turned tail and ran whenever Barlow swept through their town. Those foolish enough not to wound up with leaks in their head, courtesy of his Starr.

Barlow grudgingly admitted he admired Winston in some undefined way. The man had sand and usually Barlow would have ended his life quickly in respect of that. But a gnawing beast within Barlow reared at the challenge Winston presented. He'd not felt that rush of life since the early days, when he was still green as outlaws went, still drunk on the fever of killing and lawlessness. The bubbling of life in the veins quickly died for a man possessed of no soul. But that life was back . . . Duel Winston had revived it and more than the lust for revenge that drove John Barlow to savor his toying with the bounty man. He wouldn't kill Winston right away 'cause to do so would end the feeling and there would be nothing beyond that. Winston suffered with the knowledge his woman was in Barlow's hands and as the days trickled by the bounty hunter would slowly starve, weaken, prove less and less a threat and the cat-and-mouse game would end. For Barlow the exhilaration would die and Duel Winston would perish a beat after it.

Barlow chuckled, thinking of Winston in that saloon with nothing but whiskey and sawdust. Barlow had left the whiskey there for the express purpose of weakening the bounty hunter more. In Tumbleweed water would prove impossible to come by — Barlow reckoned he had the only canteens — and the whiskey would hasten Winston's exhaustion as it drove the sweat from his body and left him bone dry.

Barlow smiled a vicious smile. He had watched as Winston and another man left from the back of the saloon. He had let them. They would find nothing when they searched the town and that would play on Winston's nerves even more. And with what Barlow had in mind, it would be perfect to have them away from the saloon for a spell.

Barlow pondered briefly about the other man. He couldn't recollect having seen him before and he had not ridden in with Winston. He must have come in during the night. Barlow had discovered his horse at the livery and set it racing off onto the desert trail. The fellow might prove a problem, but Barlow doubted it. The man didn't look like much and Barlow'd kill him at the first opportunity.

Barlow closed the trapdoor and straightened. The chamber contained little furniture, a few bags of supplies and a rifle propped in the corner. A lantern burned low on a rickety table, throwing gnarled shadows across the ceilings and walls. Its butter glow flickered from his colorless eyes as his gaze wandered to the two women in the room.

Delaney smiled when Barlow looked at her, a vacant sense of loyalty and love showing in her eyes. Barlow ignored her and looked at Samantha Dale, who sat bound to a chair in the center of the room.

'Your boyfriend's got company, missy.' He leaned close, gripping the chair arms.

Samantha's emerald eyes narrowed. A deep-purple bruise showed on her cheek and dark circles punctuated her eyes. Her lip was swollen and her dress and bodice showed evidence of rough handling

She spat. Saliva dripped down Barlow's cheek.

The outlaw's features turned dark and he backhanded her across the jaw. Her head rocked and her teeth clacked together. Blood trickled from her lip. Her eyes glazed momentarily.

'You should be nicer to me, missy. If'n you did I could be a lot nicer to you . . . '. A lascivious glint sparked in his eyes and Samantha's face twisted with revulsion.

'Hey, Johnny, don't you go gettin' so

damn friendly with her.' Jealousy laced Delaney's tone.

Barlow's cold stare settled on her; his eyes narrowed. 'Shut up . . . ' His voice came low and threatening and Delaney took a step back. She knew better than to talk to him that way. She wasn't long for this world if she kept back-mouthing him.

Delaney stood near the corner, arms folded, eyes focused on Samantha, remaining silent.

Barlow's attention turned back to Samantha. 'Like I said, your boyfriend's got company but it ain't gonna do him a lick of good. I'm figuring on arrangin' a nice little reception for them when they get back.'

Samantha's eyes filled with spite. 'Why don't you just kill us and get it over with, you sonofabitch!'

Barlow laughed, pushing away from the chair and going to the corner. He hefted the Winchester, turning it over in his hands and sighting down the barrel.

'Why, I plan on doin' just that, missy.

But first I'm gonna play with him, make him regret the day he ever figured on doggin' me.' Barlow's gaze raked her bound form. 'I'm gonna kill you first so he can watch, but not before we have ourselves a bit of fun . . . '.

Delancy's face turned vicious with jealousy, but she said nothing. Samantha's face filled with disgust and Barlow grinned.

* * *

'You heard him,' Sam said, after Barlow had descended into the tunnel and closed the trap door.

'Whatcha say?' Delaney turned from the table she was sitting at, gazing vacantly at the lantern, deep in thought. Sam knew the dove was dwelling on what Barlow had said, the references made Sam's way. The girl loved the outlaw in some perverted sense of the word. Sam had caught the corrosive looks of jealousy Delaney cast her whenever Barlow paid her attention.

She hoped she could turn that to her advantage.

'I said, you heard what he said to me. He plans on having his way with me.'

'No, that ain't so. Johnny wouldn't do that. He loves me, ah reckon more than anything.'

Sam felt a sudden twinge of pity for the girl. She wasn't unlike a hundred other bargirls she'd encountered, ones surviving on false dreams and lives built up in their minds. The first hardcase who came along and offered them a life usually got mistaken for love, but it was almost always a case of simple use. The hardcases soon tired of the women and went on to the next. Most of the left-behinds wound up dead, by the outlaw's hand or by their own. The few who didn't were worthless from that point on. This girl had little in the way of brains and her body had been her only way of living. With Barlow she had figured on a life, whatever little that proved to be with a man like him.

Sam forced the pity down. She

couldn't let it deter her from her plan. Duel was here in Tumbleweed and Barlow planned to kill him, as well as her, and Sam would do everything she could to sop that from happening.

She eyed the dove, putting on an honest face, one she had gotten plenty of practice holding in her line of work.

'He's done it before,' Sam said coldly. The girl's face tightened as if slapped and Sam knew she had hit it right. It wasn't much of a guess; hardcases were mostly the same.

'No . . . ' the girl answered, the lie plain in her voice. She twisted her fingers into knots.

Sam pushed at the attack. 'You're lying. I can hear it in your voice. He's had other women. Lots of 'em, likely, even plenty you don't know about, I'm bettin'.'

Delaney began to look uncomfortable, fidgeting in her chair and flicking her gaze back and forth. 'Johnny loves me. He gave up them other women.'

'That so? You heard what he said to me.'

'Aw, that was nothin'. He was just tryin' to scare y'all. He just wants that man for what he done to him and I reckon that's fine with me. He'll let you go after, just y'all wait an' see.'

Sam let out a derisive laugh. 'You believe that, Delaney? If you do, you're more a fool than Barlow thinks you are!'

'Hey! You got no call sayin' somethin' lahk that. I'll make him let you go. He promised me he wouldn't kill no more after he gets done with that Winston fella.'

'How many times has he broken that promise, Delaney?' Sam could tell the girl had somehow convinced herself that Barlow's words were true and Sam had to break that trust with doubt. The outlaw had doubtlessly lied to her so many times the dove was conditioned to take his words as gospel, though the contradictory facts were always right in her face.

'He . . . ' Delaney seemed to search for words.

'He'll break his word again, Delaney. He'll have his way with me then kill me 'fore he kills Duel. You know I'm right. He's broken his promise too many times and you pretend he hasn't.'

Delaney suddenly stood, going to the corner and facing the wall. Her shoulders tightened and Sam knew she was getting her point home. She had a seed of doubt, now she had to nourish it into growing.

'You know, John Barlow's a right handsome man . . . '

Delaney spun, spikes of jealousy stabbing her eyes. Sam knew she had to play it carefully or risk getting herself killed by the dove instead of freed.

'Don't yah say that! Just don't yah say that! He loves me. He'd nevah go for the lahks of you!'

The glint in Sam's eye became sly, coy. 'No? We don't look so different you and I. We have the same color hair. Hell, bet many a man would mistake us. Who knows, maybe Johnny will like me better'n you and kill you instead . . . '

Fury exploded in Delaney's eyes, clearing away the doubt. The dove feared every word might be true, though Sam knew Barlow would never trade women. Delaney did whatever Barlow told her to do; Sam never would. Barlow knew that as well.

Delaney lunged at Sam, slapping her. The slap rang through Sam's teeth, her jaw still aching from the blow Barlow had given.

'Don' you say that! He loves me and he ain't never gonna leave me for no other woman! I'll kill him a'fore that happens!'

The look in Delaney's eyes said she would. She loved the outlaw with an almost rabid sense of dedication.

She fumbled to get her mouth working right.

'You could prevent it . . . ' she let the words ring in Delaney's ears. 'You could make sure he never falls for me.'

'How?' Delaney's fury subsided and Sam sensed she was on the verge of getting Delaney in her pocket.

'Let me go. I'll take Duel Winston far away from here and you and Johnny could live the life you always dreamed about.'

Delaney frowned. 'I cain't do that no how. Johnny would be right peeled at me if I were'n to. He wants that Duel fella to pay for his crimes.'

'Duel ain't committed no crimes, Delaney. Barlow's just looking to get me through him. He loves me, not you.'

Fury swept back into Delaney's eyes but she stood stock still. Sam saw the bargirl thinking it over, weighing the words with her limited brain power.

'You can't fool me, Delaney.' Sam cocked her head, the slyness back in her eyes. 'You want Johnny to take you away, build you a life somewhere. That ain't gonna happen long as he's got me.' Sam knew she was walking a thin line. The dove might simply decide she was too much competition and kill her on the spot. Sam had sized the dove up, figuring she wasn't really the type for killing unless pushed into it, but there was always a chance of jealous anger getting in the way.

'Yeah, yeah, reckon I do.' Delaney's eyes misted. 'Always had me this dream, you know. Had me this dream about a little place somewhere fancy, maybe San Francisco. Me an' Johnny could go there and start over, we could. I could be lahk them fancy ladies in them wishbooks. Them with their frilly dresses and parasols and high-falootin' dances. I could be lahk them, I could.'

The girl said it with such plaintiveness Sam couldn't help but feel sorry for her. 'You could, Delaney. I can see you in one of them dresses, the talk of the town. Bet all the gents would be tryin' to court you, too.'

'Don't need me no other gents: got Johnny.'

'You could have it all. You just let me go and you'll never see me or Duel again. You and Johnny could go to San

Francisco and that'd be the last of it.'

'You reckon?' A perverted sense of hope hung in the girl's voice.

'I know so, Delaney. I know so. Hell, if you keep me here, I might just decide I want Johnny for myself. I might not be able to stop myself. He's quite a fella . . . ' Sam gave a coy smile and saw the jealousy sharpen in Delaney's eyes. The girl saw her dream threatened and Sam knew she had won.

Delaney stepped over to her, going to the back of the chair and fumbling with the ropes that gouged into Sam's wrists. She felt the ropes fall away and brought her arms around. She massaged her wrists, getting the feeling back in her hands. Delaney untied her ankles from the legs of the chair. Standing, Sam felt shaky but gained strength as she moved around.

'You won't regret it, Delaney. I'm gonna get far away from here and you can have Johnny all to yourself.' And good riddance, she thought. If she could get to Duel, she would make him leave and take her with him this time.

'You don't ever get near my man, you hear that?' Delaney's eyes narrowed.

Sam nodded. 'I won't. You can be sure of that.'

Delaney nudged her head at the trapdoor. 'Go down the ladder. Take the left tunnel. Comes out at the livery. Johnny's got his horse there at the back. Y'all take it and get goin'.'

'I'll do that, Delaney.' Sam lifted the trapdoor, a twinge of guilt hitting her. She debated trying to take the girl with her, make her realize Barlow would likely be none-too-pleased she had let his prisoner go and she would be in for a beating. The guilt quickly passed. To do so might jeopardize her escape — *their* escape. She descended the ladder into the tunnel, pausing before taking the one to the left. She wondered briefly where the other tunnel led, but dismissed it and started forward.

* * *

They searched every building they could get into. Keeping close to the walls of buildings, they neared the livery. Duel felt his strength ebbing with the effort. He hadn't eaten or drunk since leaving Whitehead Pass. The heat was making him bone dry; coupled with the blood loss and dehydrating whiskey it made a dangerous combination. His strength wouldn't hold out much longer if he didn't at least get water.

Elmo appeared fresher, having eaten on the way and brought spare canteens. The canteens were the one bright spot. Elmo had left them with his horse, so with their search turning up nothing, retrieving them was the next step.

The buildings searched all proved abandoned. They held little but old furniture, dust and snakes. But no Barlow. Duel hadn't expected Barlow to make himself an easy find, but it made Duel wonder. Where could the outlaw hide? A handful of buildings, a mercantile, bank, scattered shacks, were boarded up and would take more effort to get into; those were a possibility, but Duel couldn't see it likely. All showed no sign of forced entry and no tracks indicated anyone had ever tried. Barlow needed a place of easy access and that would leave minute signs of disturbance. It left him puzzled, but the need for food and water outweighed that at the moment. As soon as he replenished his strength, he'd take a second look.

'Where the hell is he?' Elmo asked, as they approached the livery.

Duel glanced at the rooftops, the street ahead. 'He has to be here somewhere. He's got two women with him and in a town like this there ain't a lot of places to hide.'

'I heard he had some hideouts nobody knew about 'fore he turned Tumbleweed into a ghost town.'

Duel was inclined to agree. The probability had occurred to him and he'd kept a sharp eye for trapdoors and wall panels in their search, spotting none. 'That'd make our job more difficult. If we can draw Barlow into the open we have a better chance. If he's got himself holed up, our chances of getting Sam out alive . . . ' Duel let the words trail off.

Elmo's face tightened. 'We ain't out of luck yet.'

'Let's get those canteens or we might be,' Duel said, not wanting to dwell on it.

Reaching the back doors to the livery, Duel lifted the latch beam and swung the doors open. He eased the Peacemaker from its holster, the weapon strangely heavy. Pressing close to the wall, he peered inside.

The musky scent of dung, old leather and hay made his nostrils twitch. He heard a horse whinny and his gaze raked the stalls, all empty but for one on the end.

He entered the livery, shifting his Peacemaker left then right. He checked each stall, knowing any one could be hiding sudden death in the form of John Barlow.

All were empty. He recognized the

horse as the one with which Barlow had made his escape from No See, on their first encounter. The rack was empty of a saddle and supplies, so Barlow must have taken them with him. Also missing was Elmo's horse. Duel frowned, a sinking sensation in his belly.

'He knows I'm here,' Elmo muttered.

Duel nodded, holstering his weapon. 'He knew we'd come back lookin' for the canteens so he made damn sure we didn't get them.'

Elmo's face pinched. 'We'e gonna be in trouble without water. Ain't nothin' but whiskey in the Godforsaken hole and that'll dry us up quick as a sonofabitch.'

'Reckon that's the way he planned it.'

A noise grabbed his attention and he put a finger to his lips, signaling silence. The sound came again, just ahead in a middle stall, board grating against board.

In the stall the floor heaved up, hay not falling away, apparently stuck to the boards. A trap door flipped over and

Duel felt a shock of relief as Samantha Dale climbed from the opening. He helped her up, taking her in his arms and holding her tight, lost for words. He had missed her more than he could tell her and deep down had nearly reconciled himself to the fact he might never see her again. He forced a swell of tears from his eyes, and, pulling back, kissed her deeply.

'Ah hem!' Elmo exaggerated clearing his throat.

Duel drew back, peering deep into Sam's emerald eyes.

'I take it this is *her* . . . ' Elmo grinned and Duel felt a smile flicker on his lips.

'This is her.' He didn't take his gaze from Samantha's.

Sam smiled. 'Delaney's got the brains of a cowchip, thank God. I convinced her I was intendin' to steal her man and she let me go.'

'Guess your prayer worked.' Duel glanced at Elmo.

'Hope it ain't the last of 'em that does!'

'You made me a promise, Elmo. I'm callin' you on it.'

Elmo and Sam looked at Duel, puzzled.

'Take Barlow's horse and get her as far away from here as you can. Don't look back and don't stop nowhere till you get to Burton's Bend. You don't hear from me two days after you get there, move on somewhere no one can find you.' He paused. 'And Elmo . . . '

Elmo's eyes narrowed. 'Yes?'

'Take care of her.'

'Now wait just a damn minute, Duel Winston!' Anger jumped into Sam's emerald eyes.

'What about you?' Elmo quickly interjected.

'I'm stayin'. I have to. If I don't finish Barlow he'll always be there a step behind or ahead of me and someday he'll kill us all. He ain't about to let it rest after coming this far. If I know anything about the man I know that much. If I kill him you'll see me soon. He kills me, well, I'm the one he wants most. Ain't likely he'll bother you two if he don't find you right off.'

'No, it's too dangerous!' said Sam. 'I've been with Barlow long enough to know he's the closest thing there is to a devil on earth. He has the advantage.'

'Less than he had before.' Duel looked into her eyes. 'It has to be that way, Sam. I ain't about to let him have a second chance at you.'

A defiant look crossed her face. 'I ain't leavin' unless you come with us.' He saw the resolve in her eyes and had little desire or strength to argue over it.

'Sam, you have to. Barlow wants me. He won't let this be. He'll track me across hell to take his due.'

'Then I'm seein' it through with you. There ain't nothin' back in Whitehead Pass for me and there ain't nothin' for me with you dead. I won't leave without you.'

'Why don't we all leave?' Elmo put in. 'At least we'd have a chance to regroup. You need rest and water, Duel. You ain't gonna be much up to it by the time he gets around to you. We know where to find him when we want him. We can bring a posse with us.'

'You'e forgetting one thing, Elmo: there's only one horse and it ain't gonna take the three of us.'

'Then I'll stay here till you get back with supplies. You can be back in two days or less. I can hold out that long.'

A smile touched Duel's lips. He was impressed with the man's bravery. 'No, he'd kill you immediately if he got wind I'm gone and you can bet he'd notice quick.'

Elmo spread his hands. 'Then it looks like we all stay.'

9

Duel Winston, Samantha Dale and Elmo headed back to the saloon. Duel cursed the fact that Sam and Elmo weren't on their way back to Burton's Bend, but there wasn't much he could do about it. He'd spent another few minutes trying to persuade them, but neither would give in and let him deal with Barlow on his own. In a selfish way, he was thankful for their courage and stubbornness. His chances against Barlow were shrinking by the moment. He had his Peacemaker, a full load and a few spare rounds in his belt, but Barlow had God knew what for weapons and a full ration of supplies, plus Elmo's.

Barlow also had time on his side. He could afford to wait while the elements and starvation took their toll on them. Duel was in the worst shape: his mouth was dry as the desert, throat parched and raw and aching. His tongue and lips had cracked and his belly burned with hunger. Weakness was settling into his limbs and as the hours wore on, each step would grow heavier. Soon he wouldn't be able to raise the Peacemaker in defense, and soon after that delusion would grip his mind, broken only by the reality of John Barlow coming to pick his bones. Elmo would fade shortly after Duel, then Sam, who appeared the strongest. Despite Barlow's rough handling, she had been fed.

The day became scorching. The sun beat down with the ferocity of an oven, baking the land. The ramshackle buildings seemed to sway with the heat waves and the dust grew hot as coals. Duel noticed himself sweating less than he should have been. A bad sign. His body felt nearly on fire, belly somewhat nauseated. The wound on his shoulder throbbed dully. He reckoned Barlow wouldn't have long to wait.

'I ain't gonna make it much longer,

Elmo,' Duel said, as they neared the back door of the saloon. 'You gotta take that horse and ride to Whitehead Pass. Fetch the law and some canteens. I'll try to hold Barlow off as long as possible.'

'Don't seem like that's such a wise idea, Duel. I'm in better shape than you. If Barlow comes for you . . . '

Duel waved off the smaller man's words. 'Sam's good with a gun, if I recollect right.'

'Derringer,' Sam said. 'Don't know 'bout a Peacemaker.'

'Then you'll have to learn quick. Aim at the chest and pull the trigger. You'll hit something.'

'I dunno. It's gonna take me at least two days and then . . . ' Elmo frowned. ''Sides, what lawman's gonna want to come after Barlow?'

'Marshal in Whitehead Pass will if he has enough men. Tell him I need his help and to round up a posse. We got no choice. Either way we stand a good chance at dyin'. Least this way we might take Barlow with us.'

Elmo gave a hesitant nod. 'All right, I'll do it. I'll ride out right away.'

'No — tonight. You go now and Barlow will see you sure. You won't make it past the edge of town with him watching. After dark you got a slim chance. Recollect you told me you were good at sneakin' . . . '

Elmo nodded, looking none-too-pleased with losing time, but accepting it.

They reached the back alley, Duel scanning the area to make sure Barlow was nowhere in sight. He held the Peacemaker ready for the first sign of trouble.

Seeing no one, he edged back, letting Elmo and Sam go ahead of him as he covered their backs.

Elmo opened the door and stepped into the barroom.

A shot blasted and Duel started. At first he couldn't pinpoint where it had come from or where it had hit.

Time suddenly seemed frozen in the

silence following the blast. Sam stood still and Elmo seemed rooted in the doorway.

The smaller man suddenly pitched backward into Sam. She caught him, lowering him to the ground. A snake of blood wriggled from the corner of Elmo's mouth and a dark wet splotch ripened low on his abdomen.

Duel ran forward, jamming a shoulder to the wall next to the door and peering in. It took him only a second to see Barlow wasn't inside, though he had been responsible for the shot. He retreated, kneeling next to Elmo, whose mouth made silent movements.

Tears slid down Sam's face as she cradled the man's head on her lap.

'Elmo . . . ' Duel whispered, looking over the wound in the man's lower belly. A sinking sense of dread hit his stomach. The wound was serious, blood flowing liberally. The chance the bullet had hit some vital part was large.

'We gotta get you inside,' Duel said, knowing it would cause the man pain but seeing no other choice. In the position they were in, they made a perfect target if Barlow came along.

Elmo nodded, swallowing hard, eyes wide and glossy. Duel, careful as he could, slipped his arms beneath Elmo while Sam did the same on the other side. They carried him into the saloon, laying him on the floor near the bar. Sam quickly rummaged about, finding little they could use to help Elmo except a blanket riddled with holes and another bottle of whiskey.

Sam rolled the blanket and placed it under Elmo's head, then tore strips of cloth from the bottom of her skirt with the help of Duel's bowie knife. Duel sliced Elmo's shirt away from around the wound. Sickness rose in his gut.

'If it punctured an intestine . . . ' he muttered, dread stinging his heart. He had grown fond of the fake preacher and to see him this way after the courage he'd displayed made fury swell in his mind for John Barlow.

Sam's face tightened as she looked at

Duel. 'Let's hope it didn't.' She took the strips of cloth and began cleaning the wound the best she could. After dragging moments, she managed to staunch the flow of blood. It gave Duel a glimmer of hope. Still, the bullet had to come out and it was nothing they would be able to do on their own; it was too deep and in too touchy an area. Even a trained surgeon would have his hands full.

Duel lifted Elmo's head, giving him a gulp of whiskey.

'You're gonna need this for the pain,' he whispered.

'I ain't . . . gonna make it, am I?' Elmo asked in a hoarse whisper.

Duel's gaze flicked to Sam, who looked back at him with a pained expression.

'We gotta get him to a doc . . . ' She let the words fall off.

'Ain't no doc gonna come here . . . ' Elmo said, voice fading. Duel forced another slug of whiskey down his throat and the man offered a feeble smile. 'Get

. . . Barlow, Duel. Promise me that.'

'I'll get him.' Duel said it low and with fury. 'I'll get him if I have to follow him to hell.'

Sam glared at Duel, anger in her eyes, but kept silent.

Elmo's head fell back as he lost consciousness. Sam finished securing a makeshift bandage over the wound, but it would help little. Sweat beaded on Elmo's brow as a fever took him.

Duel straightened, going to a table and shaking his head in disgust. On the table, a Winchester rested on a prop frame. A line fastened to the trigger led to the handle of the back door. When Elmo opened the door, the line had pulled taut, discharging the rifle. No doubt Barlow intended the bullet for Duel. The Winchester was aimed low and likely would have taken Duel in the upper thigh or hip. Elmo, a good six inches shorter, had taken the slug in his abdomen.

Duel snatched up the rifle, examining it, checking its chambers. Slapping the weapon closed, he hurled it in a burst of anger. The rifle bounded from the wall and clattered on the floor. Sam peered at him, face drawn.

'It's empty. Barlow ain't givin' us no presents.' Duel went to the bar, grabbing the whiskey bottle and downing a deep drink. A foolish move, he knew. The whiskey would squeeze out what little water he had left in him. He slammed the bottle on the counter, muttering a curse. Again Barlow had fooled him. Now he knew why he'd seen no sign of the hardcase. Barlow had allowed them to search the town because he planned to leave his calling card, deliver one more blow to Duel Winston. Duel felt sure the outlaw intended the bullet for him and he wished to God he had taken it. Elmo would die if they didn't get him medical attention soon.

Samantha came up behind Duel and he turned to face her.

'I'll get Barlow, somehow,' he said, whiskey making his head swim.

She shook her head, anger in her eyes. 'You see that man, Duel?' She jabbed a finger at Elmo. 'You see that man? He's lying there 'cause you wouldn't give up on Barlow in the first place. It's always the same with you, Duel Winston. I should have known better than to think you'd ever change.'

'I have changed. I want to give it all up and be with you. I was coming to tell you that.'

She jammed her fists to her hips and Duel saw frustration replace some of the anger. 'But not before you went after this man, Barlow, that it? You had to do just one more bounty, you just couldn't stop.'

'I wanted the money for us, to start over — '

Her eyes narrowed. 'That's a damn lie and you know it! You wanted Barlow for yourself. You were afraid if you left something undone there'd come a day when you'd start thinkin' you made a mistake. You'd want to go back out, chase that feelin' way you did when you left me. You had to for your own foolish selfishness.'

She was right and the words cut deep. He had made mistakes, Lord knew he had, but going after Barlow made all those pale by comparison.

'I can't change it now.'

'You could have at the livery. We could have left.'

'On one horse?'

'I would have walked across hell to go away with you, Duel. We could have taken turns riding, but now we don't have that chance. Ain't likely Elmo ever will.'

'I can't change my mistakes 'cept by killin' Barlow. I have no other choice.'

'No, there's not much choice. And we'll all die for it more than like.'

Duel eyed her. 'You could still ride out tonight, get away and not look back. I ain't worth stayin' here for, Sam.'

'I will ride out tonight, Duel, because it's the only chance we got at comin' out of this alive. But you're wrong 'bout one thing; I'll always be lookin' back at what could have been if you'd let Barlow be. I'll ride back with the marshal and the doc, but if we survive by some mercy of God, I don't know if I can ever feel the same about you again. You understand?'

Duel swallowed, emotion clogging his throat. 'Reckon I do and can't blame you.' He focused his attention on the whiskey bottle, capping it, staring deep into the reddish liquor. From within the depths it all stared back at him, years of lonesomeness, death, desolation. He had come for one thing, Samantha Dale, and in his foolishness he had somehow lost her. He had no delusions what would happen when she rode off. He would likely die by the hand of John Barlow. Little would prevent that. He had his Peacemaker but couldn't hold up much longer. The heat inside him burned like a furnace and soon it would consume him. All that would be left was for Barlow to finish the job.

Sam went back to Elmo, kneeling.

The man muttered in delirium and sweat streamed down his face. Duel gave him a day, maybe a bit longer, if he weren't tended to.

The thought ate at him. This shouldn't have happened and he was responsible. Even if he killed John Barlow it would prove little consolation to his conscience.

He doubted he'd get the chance to live with the guilt.

* * *

Delaney let out a gasp as the trap door sprang open. A worried look slapped her features. She stared at John Barlow as he climbed into the room. Instantly he saw the fear in her eyes and tensed, gaze flicking to the empty chair in the center of the vault.

'Where is she?' His voice came low, threatening. His pale eyes narrowed and grew intense.

'She — she's gone, Johnny. I let her go. Now we can be together, you and me, lahk we planned.'

Fury exploded on Barlow's face. 'You let her go!'

'I had to.' Delaney's voice trembled and her eyes grew watery. 'She said she had it for you, Johnny, was gonna take you 'way from me. I couldn't let that happen.'

'You stupid — ' He kicked the chair, sending it across the room. Delaney moved back, pressing against the wall as Barlow came towards her, cold fury in his lifeless eyes.

Delaney shook her head, lips trembling. 'Johnny, please, I only meant — '

Barlow lunged, backhanding her. Her head rocked, jaw suddenly loose with the sound of a loud *snap*! She slumped, blood streaming from her lips.

'You only meant?' Barlow yelled, grabbing her by the neck and heaving her up. Her eyes flew wide in mortal terror and she gasped, choked. 'You only meant? She was my ace, you stupid whore. I wanted Winston to watch her die. I wanted him to know he caused it. Now that's all gone, ain't it?'

'She said . . . she said . . . ' Delaney's words came garbled, liquidy.

'You think I give a damn what she said? She told you what you wanted to hear, way I always do.'

'Johnny, please . . . I'm sorry . . . I'm — '

'More than you think.' Barlow squeezed her throat, cutting her words short. With his free hand he eased his knife from its sheath . . .

* * *

The situation had changed. John Barlow knew that. He made his way through the tunnel towards the livery, anger twisting his insides at the thought of Delaney releasing the girl. Samantha Dale would have been the finishing touch on his plan of revenge for Duel Winston. It made little difference in the outcome, he reckoned, but Barlow knew he had made a mistake and that irked him. He should have dealt with that useless dove that day at Morrison's jail. He had reckoned she might come in handy again but it had backfired. What the hell? Bargirls were a dime a dozen. Plenty more where Delaney had come from. Smarter even. Hell, he rather fancied that Dale girl, but turning her against Winston would be unlikely. He had planned to pay her a bit of special attention, but Delaney had spoiled that, too. He cursed the dove, the satisfaction of what he had done to her little consolation.

Barlow had known full well Delaney had let the Dale girl go. He had kept the anger seething, knowing he'd enjoy taking it out on her. He had watched from the storage closet when that fella fell into the rifle trap he'd set for Winston at the saloon. Oh, a mistake in a way, but one quickly turned to advantage. The bullet had been meant to incapacitate Winston so Barlow could simply walk in and kill the girl in front of the bounty hunter. It had worked out better in a way, prolonging the game. That other fella had taken it bad and that chipped away at Winston further. Only thing that spoiled it was the sight of the Dale girl with them.

John Barlow came through the trapdoor in the livery, tossing the canteens and saddle-bags he'd been carrying ahead of him.

The time had come to call Winston out, finish the job. The rush of life he had felt had become a stale drug and he had no reason to let Winston live any longer. He had seen the shape Winston was in and knew the bounty man could put up little resistance.

Barlow also knew Winston would be smart enough to figure out how Barlow had gotten into the saloon; he'd discover the tunnel leading to the vault. If he didn't Barlow would trap them in the saloon before the girl got the chance to ride out after dark and fetch the law.

Barlow grabbed the canteens and saddle-bags and carried them to the stall bearing his horse. He went to the bales of hay stacked near the back and pushed them sideways. His saddle and gear were hidden behind them. Hauling them to the stall, he prepared his horse to ride with the dusk. He sighed, almost regretting having to kill them; the thrill that came from it would likely never come again for him. No one would bother sending another bounty hunter after him after the famous Duel Winston was found dead in Tumbleweed, and Barlow would make certain the law got word of it. But that was the price he paid for losing his soul and he would give their deaths little more than a passing thought until he figured what town he wanted to do next.

Barlow let a laugh filter through the livery as he checked his Starr's load and holstered the weapon. He went to the doors, gazing out at the deserted street, as lifeless as his conscience. He mopped his sweat-soaked brow with a bandanna speckled with Delaney's blood and smiled.

10

'How's he holdin' up?' Duel peered at Elmo, who looked anything but well.

Sam looked up, worry on her face. 'Not good. He's lost a lot of blood and he's got a fever. He ain't gonna make it more than a day or so.'

Elmo muttered in delirium, lips quivering, sweat streaming down his face. His face had sunk and his eyelids fluttered. Duel saw any hope for the smaller man fading fast.

'He don't deserve to go like this . . . ' Duel's voice came low, hollow. He walked to the bar and leaned heavily against the counter. He felt weak, his fury for John Barlow the only thing keeping him going.

Sam straightened and came over to him, laying a hand gently on his shoulder. 'I'm sorry 'bout some of the things I said, Duel. I know that fella's being shot is makin' you hurt. And I know you never intended it to happen.'

'You got every right to say what you said. If I hadn't been so pigheaded and blind things wouldn't have ended up this way.'

'No, maybe they wouldn't have. But it would have been somethin' — some-*one* — else if not Barlow. I knew that all along but couldn't admit it to myself.' Her emerald eyes filled with resignation. 'Man like you . . . I can't live a life wonderin' if you'll ever get the urge to go chasin' ghosts every time a man like Barlow comes along.'

Duel glanced at Elmo then Sam. 'If he don't make it through the night we'll both take the horse outa here. I'll forget about Barlow.'

Sam smiled a thin smile. 'I wish that were true. But there'll be others like him even if we make it out alive. Barlow's type are like weeds. Every time you cut one down, ten more spring up to take its place. I can't live a life wonderin' if I'll wake up one morning and find you gone. And like you said, Barlow won't forget about you.'

'Reckon he won't.' He swallowed at the emotion choking his throat. She had slipped away from him and he had no one to blame but himself. 'You gotta do what you gotta do, Sam. I won't hold you to a promise you never made.'

She kissed him and he took her into his arms, holding her for long moments.

Pulling away, he looked into her eyes. 'I'm sayin' goodbye just in case . . . '

Her eyes grew heavy with sorrow, filled with tears that didn't flow. Both knew their chances of living through the day were slim. John Barlow was out there and nothing would hold him back now. Duel pushed away from the bar and went to a window, peering out through the jagged shards of glass. The midday sun glazed the dust, shimmered the air, distorted the surroundings. Tumbleweed looked like hell as sure as anything Duel had seen. And John Barlow was its devil.

He thought he saw the hardcase around every corner, yet none; on every rooftop, yet nowhere.

'He'll come soon, I reckon.'

Sam moved over to the window. 'Maybe he'll wait longer, till you get weaker.'

'Ain't much point to it, now. I'm willing to bet he knows all about Elmo and he certainly knows you escaped. Now that I got you his ace is gone and by all accounts John Barlow ain't a patient man.'

Duel scanned the street again and pushed away from the window. Barlow left him no choice. He had to find the outlaw first; it was the only chance they had. If they waited for him to come, they would be trapped. Barlow was stronger, better heeled. He also had Delaney, though Duel wasn't sure if she would resort to murder to help the outlaw but had to assume the worst.

He turned to Sam. 'Where was Barlow hiding you?'

'Bank vault, near as I could tell.

He had tunnels leading from the floor.'

Duel considered it. The bank was a few blocks down on the opposite side of the street. The livery was further still, in the opposite direction. Sam had come out of a tunnel leading to the livery, yet he felt sure Barlow would have other tunnels and other hideouts. It explained how Barlow could get into boarded-over buildings and not leave a sign.

'You said tunnels. Where did the others lead?'

She shrugged. 'There were two. Delaney didn't tell me where the second one went and I didn't stick around to find out. It went right and I went left.'

Duel nodded, something gnawing at him. He recollected the day he arrived in Tumbleweed. Barlow had allowed him to get halfway into town before taking a shot at him, close to the saloon. When Duel started running away from the saloon, lead had guided him back towards it and he'd obliged by entering. Barlow had wanted him in the saloon.

And while he and Elmo were out the hardcase had entered and set a trap. The outlaw could not have left through the back door because of the tripwire. The front? Possibly, but he would have to chance being spotted by Duel on the way back from the livery. Duel had a clear view of the street from the stable because of the angle at which the livery was set. He had seen nothing. Coldness settled in the pit of his belly.

'What is it?' asked Sam, seeing a pinched expression crease his face.

'Barlow could have killed me and Elmo at any time! That's why he was so sure of his game. He took his time 'cause he knew he had the upper hand in more ways than one.'

She shook her head. 'I don't understand.'

Duel's lips drew tight. He walked about the room, gaze searching every nook and cranny. He kicked at the sawdust and dirt on the floor, searching for the tell-tale outline of a trapdoor but saw none.

'I don't understand . . . ' He stopped, brow creasing. 'It's got to be here.'

'What? What's got to be here?'

Duel was about to answer when he spotted the storage closet door open a crack. A chill snaked down his spine. He shifted his gaze to Sam, eyes narrowing. 'That!'

'What is it?'

He gave a slight shake of his head, hand slapping to the Peacemaker in the same movement. The gun cleared leather, blasted! The bullet ploughed through the door at about waist level, slamming it shut.

Sam gasped and Duel went to the door, keeping to the side of it. Chances were slim Barlow was behind that door, but he would take no chances. Duel knew the second tunnel had to come out behind that door; there was no other place. Barlow had kept Duel in reach at every moment, probably watching him, dogging his every step.

The outlaw had known full well when Duel and Elmo left the saloon and set the trap, leaving unseen through the saloon itself. He bet Barlow had seen them carry Elmo in and knew immediately of Sam's escape. So why hadn't he killed them then? Maybe he had unfinished business.

'Delaney . . . ' Duel whispered. He gripped the handle and eased the door open. He jumped to the front and aimed into the closet. The cubicle was empty, bullet lodged in the back wall. Duel holstered the .45 as Sam came up behind him.

'Barlow knew every move we made. Reckon your other tunnel leads right here.' He knelt, running his fingers over the floorboards, finding a slim crack. He drew his bowie knife and pried at the sliver opening, lifting. The trapdoor came up and Duel peered into a dim tunnel leading under the saloon. Dull light came from somewhere beneath. He looked back to Sam, standing.

Drawing the Peacemaker again, he

handed it to Sam. She gripped it with white fingers, emerald eyes widening.

'Stay with Elmo. I'm gonna follow this and pray I surprise Barlow at the other end.'

'You'll need your gun.' Worry grew intense on her face. 'If Barlow's there he'll kill you.'

'I get the feeling he won't hang around, knowin' I'd figure it out eventually. My guess is he'll move out quick but maybe I can catch him in the act. And I ain't takin' no chance with you and Elmo this time. You see any sign of the bastard, shoot him. Anybody comes out this trap 'cept me, put a bullet between his eyes. And don't let your guard down for a second. If I don't run into Barlow first it's likely he won't bother waitin' to kill me. He'll come soon so be ready.'

'Duel . . . ' She kissed him long and deep, a kiss that tasted of goodbye. He turned to the trap entrance.

'Don't say it, Sam. We got a piece of hope and I want to hold on to that.' He started down the ladder, feeling weaker than he was willing to let on to her. Little kept him on his feet except the small burst of strength that came from the thought of surprising John Barlow.

The tunnel felt cool compared to the saloon. Thick beams supported a packed dirt ceiling. Every so often a low-turned lantern hanging from a spike driven into a wall beam lit the way.

He traveled under the main street now, halfway to the bank, he judged. He drew his bowie knife. The reports Elmo had mentioned on Barlow were accurate and Duel reckoned the hard-case had more than just these tunnels. When Barlow had fashioned this town to his liking, he had made sure he'd never be trapped. He always left himself an out, the way he had with Delaney in No See.

Ahead Duel saw the dim framework of a ladder and his heart began to thud. A welcome fear this time, none of the cold indifference that usually came over him at the end of a chase. It told him he was alive inside.

Reaching a ladder, he paused, looking up. The trapdoor gaped open. Duel wondered if Barlow were in the vault. He listened, straining to catch any sound of movement, but heard nothing. His hopes sank. Barlow had already departed. Was the outlaw already on his way to kill him? The chill inside worsened at the thought of Sam and Elmo alone in the bar-room. She had his gun and he reckoned she would have no trouble using it, but a gnawing sense of urgency plagued him.

Clamping the bowie knife in his teeth, he started up the ladder. The notion occurred to him Barlow might be waiting in the vault ready to blow his head off when he poked it through the trapway. At the top, he paused, taking the knife from his teeth and edging his head into the room, ready to jerk it back at the slightest provocation.

It wasn't necessary. He wouldn't need his knife. Barlow had gone but what he had left behind sickened Duel, told him the hardcase was even more deranged and vicious than he had thought.

He sheathed the knife and climbed into the vault.

Before him, a small table held a lantern that cast a sickly glow and glimmered from dark splatters of blood across the table top. Pools of crimson puddled on the floor. A bloody hand, fingers splayed, slightly curled, showed from the back of the table and Duel edged forward, crouching.

Delaney would never aid Barlow again. Her head canted back at a weird angle, throat sliced ear to ear, she lay behind the table. Blood soaked her front. Her eyes were glazed and wide, frozen in some horrible emotion he had never rightly seen. A look of terror, utter betrayal. Duel reached out, gently closing her eyelids. Nausea surged in his belly and bile burned in his gullet.

It occurred to him Barlow might give the girl a going over for letting Sam go, but this, this was more than Duel imagined even Barlow capable of. Duel reckoned he had played a part in that. Something about Duel's chasing him down, presenting him with opposition for one of the few times in his life, appeared to have driven the hardcase past his normal level of brutality. Delaney had been on the receiving end of it.

Duel straightened, backing away. A deep sense of grimness, the utter senselessness of violent death, weighed on him. His parents' deaths flashed through his mind. It occurred to him it was much too easy to end a life, that men like Barlow preying on the defenseless would never vanish. Had he ever thought he could stop that? If so it was a fool's errand; if not he could at least take credit for a number of innocent lives spared because he had hunted down killers, and perhaps that redeemed him, made him less guilty than Barlow.

Composing himself, Duel gave the

room a brief inspection. He spotted a pile of supplies in the corner. He went to it, locating a canteen, probably Elmo's, and uncapping it. He drank deeply of warm water, letting it soothe his swollen tongue and parched throat. He drank half the canteen, a feeling of nausea taking him, but not able to stop himself. Setting the canteen aside, he rummaged through the supplies and found a strip of jerky. He swallowed it in chunks. Not the best thing he could have eaten but better than nothing. Washing the jerky down with another gulp of water, he chewed off another piece, letting it settle in his belly.

Finished, he went through the supplies, discovering spare shells for the Winchester Barlow had left in the saloon. He pocketed them, then went to the trapway and down the ladder. He could afford to linger in the vault no longer. Barlow had to be on his way and the town of Tumbleweed would witness one more death.

He wondered whose it would be.

* * *

Samantha Dale kept the Peacemaker aimed at the storage closet, alert for any sign of movement. She prayed Duel would catch Barlow off guard and return quickly but knew that was unlikely. Men like Barlow were too crafty. But still all men made mistakes. Duel had made his and maybe Barlow was due. If Duel killed the outlaw, they could make a new life, start over.

Start over. What had she told Duel about not being able to put her trust in a life with a man who might follow the urge to leave every time a man like Barlow came along? She had lied to him and to herself if she thought that were the case. She saw no other life but that. She couldn't go back to Whitehead Pass; nothing for her there but bad memories and a life she'd just as soon leave to the past. That life was over and she would say the hell with regrets even if it meant the constant worry Duel would leave again. God knew how hard that would be, but it was more than living empty. Duel accepted her for what she was — what she *had been* — and she would have to accept him the same way.

Why are you even thinking on it? she scolded herself. John Barlow will likely kill you and Duel. That would end even a tarnished dream. Duel was on the verge of collapse and if he ran into Barlow in the vault . . .

She refused to dwell on it. Duel would find the vault empty and be back soon.

What if Barlow comes while Duel's gone?

The thought startled her. What chance would she have against him, even with the Peacemaker? Damn little, she reckoned.

She drew a deep breath and tightened her grip on the gun. By God she wouldn't make it easy on the hardcase. She was determined to fill him full of lead if he showed himself.

'Come on, Duel . . . ' she whispered,

nerves strained. She stared at the closet, frowning. Duel had left only a few minutes ago but it felt like an eternity. What had he found at the end of the tunnel? Barlow? Delaney? Death?

A sound snapped her reverie. A scuffing, like a boot across a sawdust-covered —

She whirled, dread stabbing her. A blur of movement and something cracked across her jaw! Too late she realized it was the butt of a gun.

The Peacemaker flew from her grip and she staggered, clutching to a table edge and slumping over it. A gunmetal taste filled her mouth; blood flowed from a gash where her teeth had bitten into her lip. Her senses reeled and the room whirled, shimmered, steadied. A welt of pain cascaded through her jaw; she wondered if it were broken.

Her gaze rose, blurry, but able to distinguish the devil features of John Barlow. He grinned, vicious glints dancing in his colorless eyes.

'Long time no see . . . ' he muttered,

voice low and threatening.

She spat, a mixture of blood and saliva, and he laughed as it fell short of its mark — his face.

He walked over to the Peacemaker and picked it up. Spinning, he hurled it through the open front door. 'Did you really think you could get me with that, missy? I've come too far to let you ruin my plans any further.'

'Duel'll be back anytime, now. He'll kill you.' She knew the threat sounded terribly hollow, but her mind was still hazy from the blow. She pushed herself to her feet, unsteady. Barlow looked about the room.

'Yeah? Reckon he will, but killin' me ain't part of the plan, missy. Nobody'll ever kill John Barlow. Hell, it says so in all the papers. Ain't no lawman stupid enough to come after me and I'll drive that fact home after I kill Winston.'

'You bastard!' Samantha lunged, grim courage taking her. She couldn't let him kill Duel. She collided with Barlow, gouging his face with her nails.

She managed to rake one cheek before he stopped her. He roared, bringing up his fist and sending her sprawling to the floor.

The room vibrated, revolved and blackness crept along the corners of her mind. Distantly, she heard him laughing and knew if she blacked out it was all over for her and Duel. She fought to regain her senses. Her vision cleared and she pushed herself to her hands and knees.

'Reckon I know where Winston got off to, missy.' Barlow picked up a lantern, swinging it casually. 'Right about now he's probably payin' poor Delaney his last respects.'

'Delaney . . . ' Sam muttered, stomach sinking.

'Yeah, she decided on stayin' behind. Was feelin' a bit under the weather. Reckon she won't get over it . . . ' He chuckled, pulling the chimney off the lamp. He splashed kerosene across the bartop and dug in a pocket for a lucifer. Igniting the wick, he set the chimney back on the lamp. 'You ain't about to ruin my fun this time, missy. I aim to wait till Winston gets in my sights and then kill you first. I want him to watch you die.' He motioned with the Starr.

Sam slowly gained unsteady feet and Barlow came towards her, grabbing her arm. She winced as he pulled her towards the door.

'Reckon he'll be comin' out that trapdoor any moment, now, don't you?' He peered at her, colorless eyes boring into her soul, making her shudder. 'Yeah, reckon he will. Things'll be gettin' right hot for him by then.'

John Barlow brought up the Starr suddenly and triggered a shot. On the bar, the lantern exploded, kerosene igniting in a *whoosh!* A sheet of flame raced across the bartop. Grey-black smoke billowed out like a dirty genie.

John Barlow let out a whoop and jerked Sam to the door.

'No . . . ' Sam mouthed, struggling, looking to Elmo unconscious on the floor near the door.

Barlow, seeing her intent grabbed her face in one hand, thumb and middle finger gouging into her cheeks. He pulled her face close. Sour breath assailed her nostrils.

'Your friend, he ain't gonna make it.' Barlow lifted the Starr and blasted a shot. The bullet ploughed into Elmo's chest, directly over the heart.

Sam uttered a shrill 'No!' and fought to pull away from Barlow. She knew Elmo was dead.

Barlow jammed an arm under her chin, cutting her air off until she grew too weak to struggle. 'Least he died quick.' Barlow's tone was leaden. 'Rest of you won't be so lucky.' He dragged her through the doorway.

* * *

Duel Winston smelled smoke. As he neared the saloon, wisps of smoke crept along the tunnel and his heart began to race. Had Barlow decided to try to burn them out? Was Sam trapped in the bar, along with an unconscious Elmo? Or was it worse than that?

The thought spurred Duel on. He stepped up his pace, exhausted but driven by fury and fear.

Reaching the ladder, he heard the crackling of flames from above. Smoke drifted into the opening. He clambered up the ladder, cautiously climbing into the closet, knife drawn. The caution proved unnecessary; Barlow wasn't there. Neither was Sam.

Flame engulfed the bar and thick smoke clouded the room. He spotted Elmo, a starburst of crimson across his chest. Elmo was dead; Duel could tell without going to him. A sick sensation crawled through Duel Winston. A cold rage replaced it almost immediately, filling him with strength he didn't think he had left. In the time he had been gone, Barlow had struck, killing Elmo and taking Sam. The final blow. Barlow had outmanoeuvered Duel all the way and had at the last. The edge of the bounty hunter had deserted him when he needed it most. Now there was only the slaughter. Duel fell to his knees, knife dropping from his hand as be balled his fists. He screamed in frustration and fury. He had lost the edge but he had his rage and whatever that afforded him he would take. He would die but by all that was holy Barlow would too.

Around him the heat became intolerable, reddening his face; smoke stung his eyes. Gaining his feet, he shot a gaze about the smoky room, spotting the Winchester Barlow had set the trap with. He scooped it up, loading it with the spare shells he'd found in the vault.

'You in there yet, bounty man?' a voice boomed from beyond the door. Barlow.

'Barlow, you loathsome sonofabitch!' Duel yelled, going towards the door.

'You come on out here, Winston. Slowlike or I'll kill the lady right now. 'Less you favor burnin' to death.'

Duel eyed the flames, barely aware

of the heat, now. He felt *something* . . . something familiar, the deadness at the end of the hunt, washing over him a final time. He smiled a chilled smile, emotion draining from his mind.

He went to Elmo, grabbing the man's leg and dragging him. It took more effort than he should have wasted but Elmo deserved better than burning.

Duel came out onto the boardwalk and dropped Elmo's leg.

Barlow stood in the middle of the street, Sam held in front of him, Starr's barrel jammed to her temple. He spotted his Peacemaker in the dirt, too far away for it to do him any good.

'C'mon out, bounty man. I want you to have a good look at her face when she dies.'

Duel moved out into the street, Winchester gripped loosely in his right hand, finger hooking the trigger guard.

'Let her go, Barlow. It's 'tween you and me. You're a coward to hide behind a woman.'

'Ain't a hidin', Winston. I'm usin' her, way I always use folks.'

'The way you used Delaney?' Duel tried to stall, mind feverishly searching for a way to get Sam out of harm's way. He brought up the Winchester leveling it at Barlow.

'You won't shoot, bounty man.' Barlow laughed. ''Cause you'd have to shoot through her and even the great Duel Winston ain't got the belly for that.'

'You're right on one account. I ain't got the belly for that. But you'll kill us both anyway. So what have I got to lose? You can't kill us both at the same time. Soon as you kill her I'll kill you.' Duel felt a sudden wave of dizziness take him. He had run out of time. Exhaustion had caught up with him. The fury-powered reserves had gone dry. 'Not now . . . ' he whispered, struggling to hold on. He staggered slightly and Barlow caught it.

'You ain't got nothing left, bounty

man. You won't beat me even after I kill her.'

Barlow was dead right. It was over and Duel had already lost. He fought to keep the Winchester level but it felt heavy as lead in his grip. It started to drop.

Sam screeched and kicked, taking Barlow in the shin. The outlaw bellowed and pulled the trigger of his Starr. Sam jerked her head back, slamming it against Barlow's mouth. The bullet shrieked by her forehead, barely missing.

She struggled furiously. Barlow seemed unsteady a second, kicked leg wobbly, blood streaming from his smashed lip. She jerked partially free, but he yanked her back.

Sam cleared the side of Barlow's body for a split second. That was Duel's only chance. He gripped the Winchester in both hands, fighting to steady it and pull the trigger.

Barlow saw the move and suddenly shifted the Starr in Duel's direction.

The Starr blasted first.

A bullet, hastily aimed, ripped into Duel's side. He felt himself falling, the Winchester discharging, kicking him back. The slug ploughed into the ground at Barlow's feet. The outlaw tried to aim for another shot.

The world around Duel Winston blurred, images of Sam and Barlow whirling, streaking, jerking suddenly still.

Sam renewed her struggles as the outlaw's weapon shifted to Duel, screaming and jerking from Barlow's grip.

Barlow couldn't focus on both shooting and her at the same time. She ran, diving for the Peacemaker lying in the dust.

Duel slammed to the ground with a numbness only granted those in agony. The bullet had pierced his side, the wound bleeding but not liberally. He hit the dirt on his back, Winchester propped atop him.

Sam scooped up the Peacemaker,

hastily aiming and blasting a shot before Barlow could fire at Duel.

The shot whined by Barlow and the outlaw swung his Starr in her direction. She was dead. She had no time to get off another shot and even if she had her aim was shaky and poor.

With a vicious grin, Barlow raised the gun and took a bead on her head, between the eyes. He would get his wish: Duel Winston would watch her die.

Duel forced all his remaining strength into his next move. Pushing half up, he leveled the Winchester at Barlow's chest. He had one shot and it had to be true. He said a silent prayer and squeezed the trigger.

Barlow's expression dropped and he took a funny step backwards. A storm of blood and disbelief raced across his pale eyes. He swung his gaze to Duel and shook his head slowly. In his thigh a crimson splotch expanded. The shot had gone low, but it served its purpose. It wasn't enough to drop the outlaw, who swung his gun back to finish Duel, but it was enough to pull his attention from Sam.

Duel would not have time for another shot.

Barlow brought the Starr to aim.

Two shots reverberated through the street. One came from the outlaw's gun, a reflexive shot that hit nothing. The other came from Sam. She held the Peacemaker straight-armed. Blue smoke curled from its muzzle.

A slug tore into Barlow's chest, jerking him half around. She fired again. The bullet ripped into his abdomen.

For an instant, Barlow hung suspended in place, incredulity slapping his features. Blood snaked from the corner of his mouth. He started to bring the Starr up for a shot at her, but the gun slipped suddenly from his lifeless fingers.

'You . . . ' Barlow said, a gurgle. He dropped hard face-first into the dust, clouds billowing up around him, settling over his body. His finger twitched, but that was all.

Sam dropped the Peacemaker and ran to Duel, who slumped back, gasping. She kneeled, placing his head on her lap, and kissed him.

'It's . . . over, Sam . . . now we . . . can go away together, way you always wanted . . . '

He felt little pain. Everything had a muted, numb quality and he felt blackness creeping over him.

'Shhh,' Sam whispered, placing her finger to his lips, a tear sliding down her cheek. 'We will, Duel. We will . . . '

THE END

We do hope that you have enjoyed reading this large print book.

Did you know that all of our titles are available for purchase?

We publish a wide range of high quality large print books including:
Romances, Mysteries, Classics
General Fiction
Non Fiction and Westerns

Special interest titles available in large print are:
The Little Oxford Dictionary
Music Book, Song Book
Hymn Book, Service Book

Also available from us courtesy of Oxford University Press:
Young Readers' Dictionary
(large print edition)
Young Readers' Thesaurus
(large print edition)

For further information or a free brochure, please contact us at:

Other titles in the
Linford Western Library:

A TOWN CALLED TROUBLESOME

John Dyson

Matt Matthews had carved his ranch out of the wild Wyoming frontier. But he had his troubles. The big blow of '86 was catastrophic, with dead beeves littering the plains, and the oncoming winter presaged worse. On top of this, a gang of desperadoes had moved into the Snake River valley, killing, raping and rustling. All Matt can do is to take on the killers single-handed. But will he escape the hail of lead?

CABEL

Paul K. McAfee

Josh Cabel returned home from the Civil War to find his family all murdered by rioting members of Quantrill's band. The hunt for the killers led Josh to Colorado City where, after months of searching, he finally settled down to work on a ranch nearby. He saved the life of an Indian, who led him to a cache of weapons waiting for Sitting Bull's attack on the Whites. His involvement threw Cabel into grave danger. When the final confrontation came, who had the fastest — and deadlier — draw?

RIVERBOAT

Alan C. Porter

When Rufus Blake died he was found to be carrying a gold bar from a Confederate gold shipment that had disappeared twenty years before. This inspires Wes Hardiman and Ben Travis to swap horse and trail for a riverboat, the *River Queen*, on the Mississippi, in an effort to find the missing gold. Cord Duval is set on destroying the *River Queen* and he has the power and the gunmen to do it. Guns blaze as Hardiman and Travis attempt to unravel the mystery and stay alive.